Lady Amelia Takes a Lover

a Lover

Windermeres in Love Series
Book One

Sofie Darling

ARE YOU SIGNED UP FOR DRAGONBLADE'S BLOG?

You'll get the latest news and information on exclusive giveaways, exclusive excerpts, coming releases, sales, free books, cover reveals and more.

Check out our complete list of authors, too!

No spam, no junk. That's a promise!

Sign Up Here

www.dragonbladepublishing.com

Dearest Reader;

Thank you for your support of a small press. At Dragonblade Publishing, we strive to bring you the highest quality Historical Romance from some of the best authors in the business. Without your support, there is no 'us', so we sincerely hope you adore these stories and find some new favorite authors along the way.

Happy Reading!

CEO, Dragonblade Publishing

Dedication

For Eric, always

Chapter One

Florence, Italy
March 1820

"A LL WE NEED to do is behave," said Lady Amelia Windermere for the thousandth time to her sister Delilah and cousin Juliet.

Speaking of misbehaving... Amelia turned her head this way and that and still couldn't understand precisely why the pomegranate set so prettily beneath a window refused to flow from her brush and settle onto paper like a good little watercolor.

"It's only for a little while longer," she added.

It was too much to ask that the Windermere brood behave for an indefinite amount of time. Still, she could sense eyes rolling toward the high, airy ceiling. It may have been spring in Italy, but their rented three-story palazzo held the perfect temperature, allowing gentle breezes to drift through at will. While not much was superior to her homeland England, she might have to consider that the Italian weather was. Most of England would've been soggy and cold on a late-March day like today.

"Shall we behave like Archie is behaving with his opera singer in Naples?" asked Delilah, reclining lazily across a plush velvet settee the rich hue of sunburnt earth, mischief in each syllable. Amelia didn't need to look at her sister to see it in her eyes, too.

"What happens in Naples..." Amelia wasn't quite sure where she was heading with that sentence. It was the red, she decided. The pomegranate red wasn't quite pink enough. She added a dollop of water to the paint mix.

"Stays in Naples?" added Juliet, ever a wit with wordplay and seated near the open doors that led onto the terrace. She'd positioned herself so as to better catch the afternoon light for the book she was reading.

Juliet had come to live with them after her parents had perished in a tragic carriage accident when she was but aged two years. Though a second cousin once removed, she was as a sibling and was treated as such.

"I cannot behave, Amelia," proclaimed Delilah. "You might as well toss me into the Arno now."

"Delilah," began Amelia, sensing one of her sister's dramatic moods coming on.

"What's the point of being alive if you can't truly *be alive?*"

"Delilah—"

"One's soul shrivels into nothingness."

While Juliet might have a way with creating words, Delilah had a way with speaking them. One felt perched in the palm of her hand until she'd finished. It had been so since the moment she'd strung a two-word sentence together in her baby cradle.

Still, as the elder sister by five years, Amelia knew when to put her foot down. "Delilah, I forbid you from throwing yourself into the Arno."

Her sister stared moodily out the window overlooking said river. Delilah—like all Windermeres—didn't have the natural mien for brooding, with her crystalline blue eyes and blond curls that streaked platinum in the summer sun. "My soul might demand such a cleanse." Byronic the Windermeres weren't, but Delilah was giving it her best impression.

Ever the pragmatic one, Amelia felt it her obligation to point out one important fact—the *most* important fact. "We shall never be received into polite society again."

"It would be the leap too far," said Juliet, provoking a giggle from Delilah and a reluctant smile from Amelia.

"But we *are* received in polite society," continued Juliet. Where the Windermere siblings were all curly blond hair and blue eyes, their cousin Juliet had straight black hair and clear green eyes so direct they could see into one's soul, or so it was suspected by all who met her. She had, however, inherited the famous Windermere height. They were tall to a one.

"Oh, dearest Juliet, have you learned nothing from this past year?" asked Delilah, wide-eyed and innocent. "You are speaking of polite *Italian* society, and Amelia isn't. She's speaking of the only society that matters to the English." She allowed a laden beat of time to lope past. "Polite *English* society."

"Well, I think the Italians are very nice." Juliet shrugged one shoulder and returned her attention to the book on her lap. She always had a book on her person. She even had a special necklace with a notepad attached. Juliet was serious about her words.

"Delilah," said Amelia, her brush only now making headway with this baffling pomegranate. It was the blasted texture of the thing that was trickiest to convey with a watercolor brush. "You aren't being fair to the English, or the Italians, or me. I would like to return to London and be invited to all the balls and soirées. Is that so wrong?" She glanced up. "Has the post arrived yet?"

Delilah and Juliet gave each other a sly look that said they knew exactly why Amelia had asked for the third time today. "I don't believe so," said Juliet.

The thing was Amelia had a plan to rehabilitate the Windermere reputation and slip back into the good graces of society before their parents, the Earl and Countess of Cumberland, returned from their two-year archeological journey to Samarkand. Mama and Papa need never know that their children had fled England with scandal nipping at their heels, rather than for a simple holiday.

By Amelia's calculations, that left them another year; but if all went to her plan, she and her siblings would be enjoying the highest society of the *haute ton* within three months. The plan was simple: secure an invitation to the Marchioness of Sutton's ball that marked the end of the season in early June. A cousin had assured Amelia the invitation would be arriving by post any day now. But Amelia wouldn't believe it until she held it in her hands.

And now Delilah was threatening to throw herself into the Arno.

Being the only sensible Windermere wasn't the easiest lot.

"But here's the thing, dear sister," said Delilah. "*You* want to be a lady."

"I *am* a lady." Amelia pointed her paintbrush at Delilah. "And so are *you*." Her brush shifted toward Juliet. "And *you*, too."

"I didn't choose to be a lady," said Delilah. Oh, how she loved to say that. "In fact, it's a great hindrance to what and who I want to be."

Amelia released a long-held, long-suffering sigh. "What you want to be, Delilah, is what landed you and all of us out here on the fringes of polite society in the first place."

Delilah directed her unflinching gaze at Amelia. "All you need is a paintbrush and paper to create your art."

Here came Delilah's grievance, which Amelia had heard a good seventy-three times, if once. While she had sympathy for it, she'd long lost patience with it.

"All Archie needs," said Delilah, "is a pianoforte. And, Juliet, all you need—"

Juliet held up a staying hand. As ever, she preferred to stay clear of Windermere sibling arguments. "I have no artistic talent to speak of."

"—is paper, pencil, and a chair placed at the periphery of a room for your art," finished Delilah.

Juliet's smooth brow lifted. "And what art is that?"

"Listening."

Juliet scoffed. "Listening isn't an art."

Delilah snorted. "The way you do it is, and don't think I haven't noticed." She stopped long enough to draw breath. "And *I* need a stage and an audience."

Amelia let her brush fall to the table. Now it was her turn to voice *her* grievance for the seventy-third time. "But did you need as public a one as Eton College?"

Delilah shrugged her shoulder.

Amelia wasn't finished, for her grievance was never satisfied until it had a full airing. "And did you need to pretend to be a boy pretending to be a girl pretending to be a boy to do it?"

Delilah looked at Amelia as if she'd suddenly become the most stupid woman in all the world. "That *is* the role of Viola in

4

Twelfth Night."

Amelia's eyes rolled toward the ceiling and remained there until she'd achieved a measure of calm. "But it's the bit where you pretended to be a boy to get the part in the first place that society has taken issue with."

How many times had Amelia pointed out the distinction this last year?

"Eton is an all-boys school," returned Delilah. "How else would I have been able to secure the role?"

And how many times had Delilah refused to acknowledge the point?

"And to think Archie helped you," said Amelia. She still couldn't believe it.

"The bet was Archie's idea in the first place."

"You didn't have to accept."

"Sometimes, it's like you don't know me at all," said Delilah, exasperated. "Besides, Archie's been wanting to get one over on Eton since he left however many years ago."

"But you, Delilah, are a lady of two and twenty years." How many times had Amelia pointed this out? Oh, yes, seventy-three. "How did you ever expect to succeed?"

Delilah snorted. "The haircut helped." She ran her fingers through short blond curls.

"We shan't discuss your hair," said Amelia. She still hadn't recovered from The Haircut. Delilah had once possessed the most beautiful head of hair ever beheld, rivaled only by Amelia's own long blond curls. Only Botticelli's Venus standing on her half-shell held a candle to a Windermere head of hair.

Juliet lifted her head. "I rather like Delilah's haircut."

Oh, dear cousin Juliet... So honest... So annoying.

"Lady Caroline Lamb would approve." Delilah knew precisely how to fray Amelia's last nerve.

"*I* think it makes you look like a twelfth century monk," said Amelia. "Without the bald patch, of course."

Delilah and Juliet shared a conspiratorial snicker.

"Further," Amelia couldn't help continuing, even though she really, truly shouldn't. "Lady Caroline Lamb's approval is the very last thing this family needs."

But Delilah wasn't finished torturing her sister. "I could procure a straightedge and give that bald spot a running start."

"Don't you dare." Amelia had to say it. She never quite knew how far Delilah would go.

Delilah's mouth curled into the mischievous smile that ever did get her out of trouble with her older sister. "When did Archie write that he would arrive?"

"Tomorrow." Amelia picked up her brush and resumed her study of the pomegranate. It looked...angry. Perhaps she was taking out her frustration with her family on the poor, blameless fruit.

"Which means he could arrive any time between now and next week," Juliet pointed out.

True. The Windermeres ever had a loose relationship with timekeeping.

"Oh, by the by, Amelia," said Delilah. "I've decided I shall attend tomorrow night's soirée in honor of the Duke of Ripon."

"Didn't you say soirées celebrating decrepit, old dukes weren't worth your time?"

"Don't forget *lecherous*," added Juliet. "She said that, too."

"I said *likely* weren't worth my time," said Delilah, indifferently flicking a piece of lint off her skirt. "And as none of us have ever clapped eyes on the man, as reclusive as he is, well, I'm curious, and in need of society and prosecco."

Something akin to dread filled Amelia. If Archie did, in fact, arrive tomorrow, the possibility existed that the Windermeres could be attending a society function all together—which hadn't happened since they'd left England. Which meant, of course, she would be playing nursemaid all night, because, quite simply, her siblings couldn't be trusted not to be utterly and completely themselves—charming, but improper and slightly scandalous, in either word or deed or, most like, both.

A feeling jogged on the edge of memory as if...as if she was forgetting something important, like an...

Appointment.

All-too-familiar panic seized her. "What is the time?" Time

just never seemed to pass in the linear fashion everyone said it did.

Delilah pulled a pocket watch from the discreet hip pocket she had sewn into all her dresses. She'd explained it was something about being an actress and timing and honestly Amelia hadn't been able to understand the reasoning. She couldn't bring herself to give a fig about time. Signore Rossi, her Italian art instructor, did, however.

"Five minutes shy of one of the clock."

"Blast!"

In a frantic rush that brought mean, little smiles to Delilah and Juliet's faces—they'd heard that exact exclamation regarding this very topic more times than any of them could count—Amelia gathered her brushes and palette and shoved them into her valise, which she grabbed on the run. "I'll be back in a few hours."

Muted laughter followed Amelia as she dashed from the palazzo and onto the street, her feet a rapid tattoo against cobblestones. The scents and sounds of Florence crashed into her in a frenzied rush, as they always did as she crossed one square, then another, flew down a labyrinthine maze of alleys, another square, then it was a quick turn onto a narrow street, an even quicker turn into a quiet alley. Twenty steps later, she'd arrived, panting, at the turquoise-painted gate of Signore Rossi.

Taking no time to compose herself or wipe the sweat off her flushed brow, Amelia planted both hands on the gate that led into an exterior courtyard and began to push when it suddenly gave way and an ox plowed into her, knocking her off balance and flat onto her bottom, her skirts forming a white muslin puff around her—all in the space of two seconds.

She held a hand to her forehead and glared up at the ox.

Well, not an ox, precisely. But an ox of a man, to be sure. She couldn't see his face as the sun was at his back, creating a halo of light around his massive hulking form.

"Please don't apologize," she said acidly, dusting her hands off on her skirts, before checking that nothing had spilled from her valise.

The man snorted. Rather like an ox. "That was far from my

intention. Perhaps it has occurred to you that you're entirely at fault for your current condition."

"Why…why…" she sputtered through righteous, disbelieving shock. Never in her life had she been spoken to thusly.

And she most definitely didn't like it.

He held out a hand, presumably to help her to her feet. She would rather grab hold of a writhing serpent.

Gathering the few remaining shreds of her dignity available to her, she managed to scramble to her feet with her modesty in place—*thank you very much*—even if her bottom had begun to throb. It wasn't until she was squarely facing the ox of a man— well, not *facing* precisely as he stood a good six inches taller than her and she was no diminutive woman—that a shocking fact hit her. "You're an Englishman."

And a noble one at that, given the clipped syllables of his speech, even if his appearance lent a different impression given that he was wearing the clothes of a laborer and his brown hair hung unfashionably long and loose about his face.

What sort of English nobleman was this ox anyway?

He grunted—like a grouchy Highland coo she'd once encountered in Scotland—and that was leave taken as he brushed past. A faint blend of scents remained—clove, sandalwood, and… Was that *sweat*?

Tetchy remnants of the encounter quaking through her, Amelia entered Signore Rossi's exterior courtyard and halted, dipping a hand into the fountain depicting frolicking water sprites and bringing it to her face. She needed a quick cool-down before greeting Signore. What just happened?

Servants accustomed to her twice-a-week arrival simply nodded as she slipped through Signore's typically Italian palazzo and into the studio, with its tremendous north-facing windows that allowed light to pour in at all hours of the day. She found her customary easel and began readying her pencils and brushes. A bowl of fruit had been arranged for her session today. Perhaps not the most exciting subject, but a useful one in her education, of course.

Still, how many bowls of fruit had she painted in her life?

The lot of the gentlelady painter.

Signore Rossi and his little white dog Dolce entered the studio. "Ah, Signorina Amelia, you decided to join us today." He ever commented on her lateness—as was his rightful prerogative—but did so with a smile on his face.

Dolce curled up on his purple velvet pillow across from her, allowing sunlight to soak into his scruffy white fur, his little face resting on a paw, gaze lazily fixed on outdoor happenings in the cypress trees. Amelia found herself doing a sketch. Just a few lines to expand upon later.

Signore glanced over her shoulder. "Ah, would you like to paint Dolce today?"

"*Si*," she said, already delighting in the prospect. She rarely painted live forms with Signore.

She attempted to quiet her mind and enter the creative space where her brush would find inspiration for this little moppet of a dog. But she was still fizzing with her collision with the ox. Before she knew it, words were spilling from her mouth. "I just had the most curious encounter at the entrance to your studio."

Signore Rossi didn't bother looking up. "Hmm."

"With the most incredibly rude man."

A name, she wanted a name.

All Signore gave her was another, "Hmm."

She wasn't to be put off so easily. The ox was a menace and an Englishman. She couldn't let it pass. "Is he your student?"

She had to know.

Even as the question passed her lips, however, an image entered her mind. Of his hands, unrepentantly massive and masculine, like the rest of him. She couldn't imagine those hands holding anything as delicate as a paintbrush. Surely, it would snap in two.

Signore Rossi set his charcoal down and gave her an indulgent smile. "Signorina Amelia, would you appreciate me passing your information along to all manner of those who might ask about you?"

There was but one answer, and it put her in her place. "No."

Signore nodded, and that was her question sorted. She wasn't to know. She was to forget the ox of an English nobleman whose face she hadn't clearly seen.

Dolce shot to his four feet and gave a sudden round of barking at the squirrel who had the temerity to race up the cypress nearest the window. The little dog was on high defensive alert.

A chirrup of giggles escaped Amelia, and her brush sparked with inspiration. She would call the painting, *Our Greatest Defender*.

As her brush followed the creative muse where it led, oxes of men were forgotten.

For now.

Chapter Two

Next day

RED CLAY MOVING beneath his fingers, alternately resisting and bending to his will—the line of a clavicle here...a curve of a hip there, flowing into the long length of a feminine leg—Tristan sank into the feeling of creation that never failed to bring him deep satisfaction. Not much rivaled the experience of molding human form from sticky dirt.

Perhaps the invitation in his model's dark, doe-like eyes.

An invitation he must refuse.

"Our session today will be a short one," he said, blunt. He wasn't one for small talk.

"A short one?" asked the model, an Italian principessa with a penchant for sculptors. She was lush and curvy and utterly spoiled and entirely accustomed to getting her way. "But you, *mio amante*, specialize in long sessions—*very* long."

He glanced up, impatient. "Not tonight." He really wished she would stop moving. "I must attend a soirée."

Her full lips formed into a pout. "You don't like large gatherings of people. From my experience, you much prefer a small gathering of two. *Alone.* Preferably with a soft surface somewhere near."

Tristan snorted. She wasn't wrong. Even so... "It happens this soirée is being held in my honor." That would teach him to spread his money around with endowments for schools.

The principessa licked her lips and tossed her glorious head of sable hair. "I want you to place those big hands of yours on me and make love to me all night."

"Not tonight."

She must've heard the implacability in his voice, for in an instant, her pout turned into fury provoked by denial. She bolted upright on a huff, grabbed her discarded gown, and marched across the studio where she dressed in the haphazard manner of one unaccustomed to dressing herself. Of course, she had servants for that.

Tristan could be a gentleman and assist her, but he hadn't come to Italy to be a gentleman. He'd come here to be an artist, and right now the muse was flowing.

Still, he maintained half an eye on her. Best one kept watch on an angry lover, a maxim borne from painful experience. Some ladies possessed right good throwing arms.

"I come first or not at all," the principessa hissed at him as she jerked the door open. He should probably mention that the buttons of her dress didn't line up and her right breast looked in danger of spilling from her square-cut bodice. He'd leave her unintended double entendre unmentioned, too.

Instead, he snorted.

She gave a tiny roar of frustration and slammed the door behind her. He'd rather she'd left it open for the light breeze that always picked up in late afternoon. Still, relief swept through him. His relations with the principessa had reached the point that he would rather deal with the facsimile of the woman—in this case a clay statue—than the actual flesh-and-blood woman.

It was the inevitable end, for like every woman he'd known, she had her demands. Most of them he could fulfill to both their satisfaction, save one—the one that ever proved the breaking point.

That he set her on a pedestal and adore her.

It wasn't that women weren't worthy of adoration.

It was that no one was.

Weren't they all human with wants and needs? All in search of that kernel of the ineffable that could make them happy? And if not happy, then fulfilled?

Becoming enslaved to another wasn't the way to achieve that

outcome.

He grabbed a large towel and dipped it into a drum of water before draping it over the sculpture to prevent it from drying out. He would be lucky if the principessa let him finish.

It wouldn't be the first time he'd lost a mistress in the middle of a sculpture. Nor would it be the last, he suspected.

Truth told, the charity soirée didn't figure into Tristan's equation for fulfillment, either. In fact, he resented the world outside his studio for intruding into his life.

After all, he'd chosen this estate on the outskirts of Florence for a reason. Well, several reasons. The house was set on top of a hill, which allowed the breeze through at all hours. His studio was separate from the house, so he didn't have servants banging about all day—Cook was a whistler. But the most important reason was its seclusion. Not a single aristocrat—English or otherwise—within a mile.

But, of course, he'd had to go and throw money around to help the less fortunate, and the aristocrats had noticed. No good deed went unpunished.

Then he'd had to go and donate to a charity raffle. The Contessa di Mapelli, who was organizing the soirée, had informed him of a children's school a few miles beyond the outskirts of the city that had a leaky roof. Before he knew what he was saying, he'd volunteered to sculpt a bust of a raffle winner and, further, to supplement the monies raised to provide an entirely new building for the children.

The donation itself, he didn't mind. But he would also be paying with something more precious: his time. He would have to spend time with the lucky aristocrat who won tonight's raffle, which would eat into his remaining six months in Italy.

And he only had himself to blame.

He lifted the cloth off the sculpture. As he walked around the pedestal, viewing it from every angle, his mind's eye struggled to recapture a picture of the principessa in repose, lush and desirous. Instead, an altogether different image insisted on pushing in: *a woman...tall and willowy of form...English elegance... Outraged eyes staring up at him from the ground, her skirts billowed about her...*

Strangely, he found himself wishing the woman had accepted his hand to assist her to her feet. He wanted to peel away her kidskin glove and know the feel of that hand. The flesh. The sinew and bone beneath. Hers would be a slender, elegant hand possessed of steel, like the rest of her, he suspected.

He gave his head a clearing shake, dismissing the image and the woman. He'd come to Italy to escape her sort— *English...proper.* Now, he had but a mere six months before he would return to the soggy shores of his homeland and resume his rightful place in its hierarchy. He wouldn't waste that time thinking about proper Englishwomen with blue eyes that sparked with fire and hair that shone platinum in the sun and whose curls only awaited a light breeze to become unruly.

No, he wouldn't think about that woman at all.

Instead, he would attempt to bend a stubborn lump of clay to his will for a while longer, before closing up his studio for the evening.

Then he would try to make himself presentable for a gathering of his peers. He wasn't sure he even knew how anymore.

He might have gone entirely to seed.

⚜

WELL, PERHAPS NOT entirely gone to seed, Tristan thought as he stepped inside the contessa's ballroom presently accommodating a few hundred of her closest friends. In fact, it might be possible that he cleaned up well enough for decency's sake.

Still, he hadn't felt this grouchy in a good number of years. Four and a half, to be exact—since he'd left England.

"Ripon, your smile is slipping," said the Contessa di Mapelli, or Bianca as she preferred to be called. Her arm twined through the crook of his. "Walk the room with me."

"I never did learn the knack of it," he said.

"The knack of walking?"

"Smiling."

This provoked a girlish laugh from the contessa. "You simply haven't met the right woman." She swept her closed fan in a wide arc. "Perhaps she is in this very room tonight."

"Are you propositioning me, Bianca?" he asked, flirtatious. Perhaps he hadn't gone to seed at all.

She gave his arm a light swat. "If I were a few decades younger, none of these other ladies would stand a chance. Now, paste a smile on your face. The Earl of Inesley promised funding for a mural restoration a year ago, and now we must shame him into turning promises into coins."

As they wended their way through the room toward their quarry, Tristan couldn't help noticing the way his countrymen and women observed him—like an escaped zoo animal who needed to be returned to his cage. But, really, could he blame them? After all, it had created quite the stir when his fiancée, Lady Sarah Locksley, had jilted him. Except…

Was it a jilting if the split happened three days before the wedding? He wasn't sure, but that was how he referred to the event in his mind. *The Jilting*. Not that it hadn't been amicable on his part—and a relief. Lady Sarah, however, hadn't felt quite so sanguine.

The contessa located her prey and commenced her public shaming with a generous smile on her face. Tristan settled back and appeared entranced by her every word. As he had no intention of engaging in small talk this evening, he found monosyllabic grunts to be effective in staving off attempts.

In truth, he hadn't been prepared for the sheer number of his compatriots in one room, many of whom regarded him with knowing cuts of the eye or sharp little smiles about their mouths. They were curious about him. Which was to be expected, for Lady Sarah had sullied his name to anyone who would listen, electing not to leave the reason for their split a mystery. Truly, the *ton* loved nothing more than to form their own interpretation of events that had naught to do with them, but she'd chosen the opposite course and branded him a knave.

Perhaps he was.

Yet he refused to bear her any ill will. After all, the whole kerfuffle was the impetus he'd needed to leave England and seek broader vistas on the Continent. Really, she'd given him the gift of four and a half of the best years of his life.

"Move with me, Ripon," said the contessa.

"Are there others in need of a good shaming?" he asked.

The contessa's mouth curved in a feline smile. "Always."

As it was done in the cause of charity, Tristan didn't mind being party to the contessa's coercive tactics. There might not exist a stingier creature than the English nobleman.

As he escorted the contessa to another grouping, a vision of his very near future flashed before him. Of him navigating versions of this exact same soirée four nights a week for the remainder of his days once he returned to England.

His life would forever be divided into before, during, and after Florence. He wasn't much looking forward to the *after*. But he'd cut a deal with Mother, and he would honor it like the gentleman he hadn't much use for being.

Frustration spiked through him. So, why was he currently in a Florentine ballroom full to bursting with English lords and ladies? Wouldn't he be seeing these same bland faces in six months' time anyway?

The blasted English kept flocking to Florence.

And finding him.

And drawing him back into their world.

That was why.

He'd escaped his fate these last four and a half years, but he would succumb and be theirs again.

Soon.

"If it isn't Ripon," called a voice growing closer with each syllable.

Tristan's head whipped around to find a tall, lean man of thirty-odd years approaching. *Lord Daniel Windermere, Viscount Archer.* Known to all as Archie, he was gaining ground at his customary rapid clip—the man didn't know how to move any other way—and with a devil-may-care smile on his face. He didn't know how to smile any other way, either.

At last, someone Tristan actually didn't mind seeing. Though Archie was a few years younger, Tristan had always liked the lad when their attendance at Eton had overlapped. Always on the prowl for a good time, Lord Archer was. He was known for it.

The men gave each other great manly claps on the back as Tristan asked, "What brings you to Italy, Archer?" He didn't quite feel on "Archie" terms with the man.

"Oh, you know, women," said Archer on the laugh ever ready on his mouth.

Tristan snorted.

Archer gave his head a rueful shake. "Not that sort." He cocked his head. "Well, mostly not that sort. Women of the familial variety."

"Ah," said Tristan as if he understood. He didn't. He'd never paid much attention to Debrett's, therefore knew nothing of Lord Archer's family. He did seem to remember eccentric parents, though.

Someone caught Archer's eye, and he jutted his chin. "Like *that* someone."

Across the gleaming mahogany parquet floor stood a lady who might be the tallest woman present. *Willowy...elegant...and possessed of blonde hair that longed to be loosed from its staid chignon and set free into wild, unruly curls...*

Her.

Tristan felt his brow crinkle. "Who is that woman?" he asked. He might've demanded.

"That *lady* is none other than one of two of my sisters," said Archer.

Of course. She had the Windermere look.

"*Amelia,*" Archer called out.

Her shoulders tensed. She'd heard her brother. There wasn't any way she couldn't have. Half the room had heard, and turned.

Except her.

She was very clearly attempting to ignore her brother.

Even Tristan knew that wouldn't work. Unafraid of making a scene, Archer wasn't the sort of man to be ignored.

Archer cut Tristan a quick smile that teetered on the other side of audacious. "I'll introduce you to my sister. She absolutely cannot stand improper introductions. Or improprieties of any sort, really. Sometimes, I feel she's deserving of our pity, being born a Windermere, you know. It can't be easy if all you want is the straight and proper path."

Tristan knew he should beg off and attend to his hostess, but he found that he very much wanted to be introduced to this Amelia. *Lady* Amelia, as she was the daughter of an earl.

Archer gave his throat a loud clearing. *"Amelia."*

Well, that secured the other half of the room's attention. No longer could Lady Amelia deliberately disregard Archer. He'd made it impossible. She pivoted in a whirl of swishing peacock-blue skirts and glared at her brother as only a sister could. With a face like a Fury, she crossed the room, shoulders squared, with her dignity held intact. Admirable, really. Tristan found himself anticipating his official introduction to this Lady Amelia.

She'd opened her mouth, surely to launch into a blistering scold of her brother, when she spared Tristan a quick glance. The contact lasted no longer than the split of a second. A little crease formed on her brow. Her gaze flew toward him again and settled, teetering just on the edge of recognition.

He knew precisely how to tip her over. He gave a shallow bow and said, "His Grace the Duke of Ripon, at your service."

Her eyes widened into saucers. She hadn't known his name, but his voice, she would've remembered.

He watched in fascination as a riot of emotion marched across her face in quick succession—*shock...horror...disbelief*—before settling on utter befuddlement.

"*You,*" she gasped. "*You* are the duke?"

Tristan had begun to enjoy himself. Unexpected, that. "*I.*" A beat. "The duke."

"*You* are the old, decrepit Duke of Ripon?"

Old? Decrepit? He was a virile four and thirty years, if he said so himself. "Perhaps to some?" he allowed.

"*You* aren't old." She swallowed. "Or decrepit."

Her gaze remained fixed on him as if he were an oddity descended from the far reaches of the universe. Was it so very odd that he was a duke?

She wasn't finished. "How on earth can *you* be the duke? You're an ox."

He snorted. "Oh, I can assure you I'm most definitely a man." He shouldn't say what next wanted to fall from his mouth... "I can prove it if you like."

A too-loud guffaw burst from Archer. "Well done, old chap."

Tristan hardly noted it. His attention was entirely fixed on the lady before him—the one currently blushing from the tips of her ears to the tips of her toes.

Good.

She looked like the sort of young lady who could use a good blushing every so often.

He could think of a good something else she could be in use of, too.

And how he wouldn't mind very much giving it to her.

Chapter Three

I CAN PROVE it if you like.

Had the ox—who was *impossibly* the *Duke of Ripon*—truly spoken those words to her?

She ought to…she ought to…

Amelia clenched her fists at her sides and stamped her foot.

All that seemed to do was amuse him, judging by the glimmer in his eyes.

She didn't know how to respond to such words. They sparked outrage, of course, but something else, too. A funny little feeling that crept through her, leaving a trail of heightened sensation, making her a trifle winded.

"I say," said Archie, her trouble-making, disloyal brother who should be challenging the duke to a duel instead of snickering, "do you know each other?"

"No," Amelia responded, too quickly. She sounded like she was lying, which of course, she was. Both Archie and Ripon quirked an eyebrow. Oh, she needed to get away from these men.

She directed a shallow curtsy in the direction of the duke. "Meeting you was certainly—"

Awful. The worst thing to happen to her since she left England. But she couldn't say that. Not in polite company, anyway.

So, she pasted the smile reserved for polite company onto her face and finished with, *"Diverting."*

The man snorted.

The absolute cheek.

She swiveled in a flurry of skirts, her ears clouded with a strange sort of fury. Why did she let the man upset her so? It was simply that he was so very rude.

But was it rudeness?

Yes. But something else, too.

Honesty.

She couldn't understand it. Who ventured into society with honesty?

Everything in her rejected the very idea.

The unstated social contract demanded that the *haute ton* gather at balls and soirées and musicales and fêtes with smiles on their faces and platitudes on their mouths, and if not platitudes, then gossip. In short, it was all a great big game of pretend and the important thing was that they all agree to play by the rules. But people like the Duke of Ripon and—it had to be admitted—Archie, and sometimes Delilah, acted as if the rules didn't apply to them.

Rules applied to *everyone*, that was what Amelia had learned this last year. Rules didn't go away because one didn't like them or chose to ignore them. Instead, they lurked in the shadows and waited patiently for their opportunity to strike and punish when one fell afoul of them.

Amelia snatched a cup of punch off a passing tray and took a cooling sip. The cotton in her ears cleared, and she thought she might've heard her name.

She glanced around to find a group of ladies staring at her. She knew a few of them vaguely, but none well. Or not well enough for them to be desirous—a few looked shockingly *eager*—for her company.

"Is your brother an intimate of the duke?"

"The duke?" she asked, momentarily flummoxed.

Her audience stared at her as if she was the biggest dolt in this—or any other—room.

"Of *Ripon*."

Oh, *the ox.* "I'm not sure."

"Or are *you*, perhaps?" giggled one of the ladies.

Amelia's cheeks shot into instant flame. "I can most definitely say *no* on that point."

A few of her audience looked disappointed, others plainly curious. "But why would you want to say no?"

Amelia gasped before her mouth snapped shut. Sometimes she forgot she wasn't in England. In Italy, lovers were allowed, if one stayed discreet. She couldn't allow such mores to rub off on her, or on Delilah and Juliet. She glanced around. Where were they anyway?

She was about to excuse herself when one of the ladies said, "Didn't you know his fiancée left him at the altar?"

Amelia's feet remained exactly where they were.

She shouldn't listen, but she was, *oh*, so very curious about the ox. And if knowledge came in the form of unreliable gossip, so be it. After all, where there was smoke, fire often followed.

"What woman would jilt such a man?"

Every eye—including Amelia's, shamefully—swung toward him. Of a sudden, the path between them and him cleared, allowing an unimpeded view of the Duke of Ripon. He looked every inch the English duke of novels that Amelia only read in the privacy of her bedroom. Thick, tousled sable hair. Gray eyes that pierced. Clean-shaven, square masculine jaw. Purely from an artist's point of view, the man was devastatingly handsome.

"It is whispered he told his fiancée she could take lovers," whispered one lady.

"Why would she need to?" asked another.

An appreciative silence followed.

"They say he has no morals."

"The Dissolute Duke."

Amelia suspected she was alone in finding amorality and dissolution to be negative qualities in one's husband.

"Of course, he came to Italy."

A round of snickers followed.

"But *you* came to Italy," said Amelia for some reason she couldn't fathom.

One lady with a particularly wicked smile held Amelia in her cool gaze. "*Esattamente.*"

That was Amelia put in her place. This time, the snickers directed at her sounded no small amount mean-spirited. She might've been one of them according to Debrett's, but she wasn't one of *them*, the hard glints in their eyes seemed to say.

She gathered the shreds of her dignity about her—she seemed to be doing that a lot lately—and aimed her feet for the ladies' retiring room. She needed a moment to herself. She'd made it no more than halfway to her destination when she heard, "*Amelia.*"

She turned to find Delilah and Juliet fast approaching.

"Dearest sister, you're as pale as a sheet," said Delilah. "What is it you're drinking?"

"Punch."

"That would explain it," said Delilah, waving a server over. "You're in need of something stronger."

"I can assure you I am not."

"Like prosecco." Delilah lifted two glasses of the bubbly spirit off a silver tray.

"Young, marriageable ladies do not drink prosecco at soirées," said Amelia, refusing to accept a coupe.

"They do in Italy," observed Juliet.

"Besides, you're seven and twenty, dear sister," said Delilah, taking a delicate sip. "You're too old to be young."

"Delilah!"

Her sister wasn't finished. "And as far as marriageability goes, it might be fair to say you're on the shelf."

"Only until we return to England," said Amelia, defensive.

"And what did you call it before then?"

"I simply haven't met the gentleman who suits me." Before Delilah could voice more opinions on the matter, Amelia added, "*Yet.*"

Delilah and Juliet exchanged one of their looks.

"Did you know Archie arrived?" asked Amelia.

"Oh, yes," said Delilah, "with his great lumbering Scottish friend, Rory."

"Lord Kilmuir," corrected Juliet.

Amelia cared not either way. "I didn't notice him." She'd only had eyes for the ox.

She wouldn't be speaking that last part aloud.

"Come," said Delilah. "Let us look at the offerings for the raffle."

Twenty minutes later, between the three of them, they'd bought tickets for items ranging from a Lagotto Romagnolo puppy to a marble bust carved by a local sculptor.

"How could we have bid on every single item?" asked Amelia.

"They make it remarkably easy," said Juliet. "You simply write your name on a card and splash out the blunt."

Amelia resisted the urge to roll her eyes toward the ceiling. "I know how raffles work, Juliet, but, really, do any of us need a stone bust?"

Delilah shrugged. "You're only young once, so may as well immortalize it in stone."

"I thought I was no longer young."

"Well, you've been old since the day you were born—"

"That'll be quite enough."

"Oh, I almost forgot," said Delilah. "Did you meet the old, decrepit duke?"

Oh. This subject. "Um, yes."

"Is he a complete lech?"

"Possibly."

Likely.

Delilah craned her head to better scan the room. "Well, where is he?"

It didn't take long for Amelia to find him engaged in conversation with no fewer than eight ladies. A strange feeling tingled through her. The same uncomfortable one from earlier.

"*There.*"

Delilah and Juliet followed the jut of her chin. Juliet's eyebrows shot upwards, and Delilah's jaw fell to the floor. "*That* is our old, decrepit duke?"

"Um, yes."

"*Oh, my,*" exhaled Juliet.

Again, leave it to Juliet to sum up a situation perfectly.

Delilah lifted another two coupes of prosecco off a passing

tray and again tried to hand one to Amelia. She gave her head a decided shake. Delilah shrugged and began alternating sips between the two coupes. Juliet giggled. Which was all the encouragement Delilah needed. Perfect peas in a pod, those two. One in need of an adoring audience; the other only too happy to provide it.

Ding-ding-ding. The sound of metal tapping crystal, calling the gathered's attention to a low stage set before the large bow window overlooking the back garden. The raffle began, which meant this interminable night was—*blessedly*—nearing its end.

Juliet won two items—a length of Brussels lace and an enameled snuffbox—and Delilah won one—a silver brush and mirror set. Thankfully, someone else got the puppy. With only a single item remaining Amelia began encouraging Delilah and Juliet toward the door.

Then it happened.

Her name was called.

People began staring at her, as if they expected something. Delilah gave a quick jerk of her head in the direction of the bow window.

Finally, it hit Amelia. She'd won the night's grand prize, and she was to accept it before all.

Oh, she didn't like that one bit.

The sharp point of Juliet's elbow nudged between her ribs to get her moving. The Contessa di Mapelli waited with a patient, regal smile on her face. But it was the person standing beside the Contessa who claimed all Amelia's attention. *Him*—the ox...the Duke of Ripon.

Dread clawed its way through her. Why was he regarding her with that expression on his face? As if he were experiencing the same foreboding as she?

Once Amelia finally reached the low stage, the contessa said, "Lady Amelia Windermere, our grand prize winner. Thank you to all who generously donated of your pounds tonight, I look forward to receiving notes from each and every one of you." *And if you don't pay up,* her smile seemed to say, *I know where you sleep.*

An awkward smile on her face, hands clenched at her sides,

Amelia cut the duke a quick glance. Why was he staring at her like that?

"...and a bust done by no other hands than those of the Duke of Ripon."

Amelia blinked. What was the contessa saying?

She met the duke's gaze. He simply kept staring at her.

And she understood.

"I...I..." she stammered. "I cannot possibly accept such a"—*terrible...awful...horrifying*—"*generous* gift. Perhaps I could donate it—"

"As you English say, *pish*," dismissed the contessa. Was that a glint of mischief in her eyes? "The bust is yours, fairly won."

"But, truly, I cannot—" The rest of the sentence died in Amelia's mouth when she gazed out upon the gathered. That was definitely mischief shining in Delilah's eyes. Juliet's, too. And the other ladies? To a one, they glared at her with false smiles on their mouths and envy in their eyes. This wasn't a crowd sympathetic to her predicament. Perhaps the duke—

He was no help.

He simply observed her as if from a safe distance.

She was on her own.

She smiled graciously, thanked the contessa, and stepped from the platform, the blood rioting through her veins. She kept going hot, then cold, then hot again as she moved trance-like through the crowd that was now dispersing.

His gaze...it was upon her.

It hadn't once left her, she knew it. And it wouldn't until she was gone from the room.

She knew that, too.

Her step quickened. She couldn't think properly with that man's gaze upon her.

Delilah and Juliet filed in behind her as they stepped from the contessa's palazzo and into their waiting carriage.

The dazed feeling began to dissipate, and Amelia's first clear thought of the evening was allowed entry. She could let the contessa keep her money and beg off, couldn't she? No one would be the wiser, except for her and the Duke of Ripon. But the way he'd been observing her...

Was that interest she'd detected?

Perhaps he wouldn't let her beg off.

Strange thought.

And perhaps she wouldn't want him to.

Stranger thought, still.

The carriage lurched into motion, and her gaze flew up to find Delilah and Juliet staring at her from their bench opposite. They had something to say.

It was Delilah who said it. "Do not even think of begging off."

Chapter Four

Next evening

"**I** SHAN'T SIT for the bust," said Amelia with the certainty of one who knew for a fact that she occupied the moral high ground. "It wouldn't be—"

"*Proper!*" shouted Archie and Delilah from their end of the long dining table that could easily sit thirty, but tonight sat only five—the Windermeres and Lord Rory Macbeth, current Viscount Kilmuir and future Sixth Earl of Carrick.

Amelia resisted the urge to roll her eyes toward the half-lit chandelier. Those two ever delighted in teaming up against her. Juliet smiled down into her soup, and Kilmuir stared morosely out the window. Apparently, his proposal of marriage had been turned down by Miss Davina Dalhousie, and he was having difficulty reconciling himself to the fact. Actually, the *ton* being the close-knit society it was, the Windermeres and Dalhousies had long been family friends, and while Amelia had never been close to Miss Dalhousie, who was several years her junior, she knew the young lady to be possessed of a clear head and good sense. And Kilmuir…

He'd always been perfectly amiable and pleasant and quite handsome to gaze upon with his top of golden red hair and clear blue eyes—the thought had even crossed her mind that Juliet might harbor a slight infatuation for him—but…there didn't seem to be all that much more to him. In other words, Amelia doubted not that Miss Dalhousie must've had a good reason for refusing a proposal of marriage from such an eminently eligible gentleman.

Speaking of refusals of marriage from eminently eligible gentlemen...

Amelia's gaze shifted and landed on Delilah. "You know, Delilah," she began, settling back to allow a servant to remove her soup bowl, "you received a perfectly good proposal of marriage from Mr. Oliver Quincy."

Having only just eaten her last spoonful of soup, Delilah nearly succumbed to a coughing fit. She held up a finger and downed several unladylike gulps of water before clearing her throat on a loud harrumph. "Perhaps the Italian heat has muddled your brain, Amelia," she said, her voice scratchy. "There was and is nothing *perfectly good* about that marriage proposal."

"Oh, come now," said Archie, no mistaking the tease in his voice, "just imagine spending the rest of your days in worship to a man who loves nothing more than to pontificate about the nobility's right to rule or the importance of achieving a perfect knot on one's cravat."

Delilah primly wiped each corner of her mouth. "I don't believe I shall."

"By the by," said Archie, "we'll have guests for supper."

"Just tell me the night," said Amelia, "and I'll arrange it with the servants."

"Oh, well, that's easy." Archie smiled the too-charming smile she knew to be wary of. "Tonight."

Amelia willed the patience of Job into her response. "But supper has already begun, Archie."

"I'd forgotten you eat when it's still daylight."

Amelia ignored the jibe. "And who are these guests?"

"As it happens, one is Ripon."

"The Duke of Ripon? *Here?*" The very idea walloped Amelia over the head. *The Duke of Ripon?* In *her* home? "Oh, Archie, why have you gone and done that?"

"The man is a legend," he said, as if that explained it.

It explained nothing.

"From the gossip about him last night," said Amelia, "it's quite clear the man is a *scandal.*"

"*We* are a scandal," said Delilah with no small amount of glee.

Which was exactly why they needed to distance themselves as far away as possible from the man. Did her siblings understand nothing?

"Ripon is a scandal *and* a legend," said Archie.

Before he could regale them with the legendary exploits of the Duke of Ripon—and, in truth, Amelia was just a wee bit curious—in strode a tall, striking man known to all in the room. *His Grace Sebastian Crewe, the Duke of Ravensworth.* Amelia reckoned he was the other guest that Archie hadn't yet mentioned.

Two dukes to an informal supper.

Only in Italy.

"Seb," said Archie, standing and giving his friend a great clap on the back before indicating Ravensworth take the seat beside him. Amelia gave a servant a quick instruction to set the duke's place for supper.

The instant Ravensworth sat bottom on seat, Delilah shot to her feet, her chair nearly toppling over behind her. Without a word, she marched from the room in a fury. One never knew what form Delilah's moods would take from one moment to the next.

"Actresses," said Archie, dismissive.

"I'm certain it's nothing to do with you personally," said Amelia, as ever smoothing over the ruffled feathers left in her siblings' wake.

"Oh, it has everything to do with me personally," said the duke, unfussed, his gaze lingering on the doorway Delilah had disappeared through. "Further, I can't blame her for seeing herself as in the right."

A beat of silence followed, but Ravensworth clearly didn't feel the need to elaborate, and no one could make a duke expand on a topic if he chose not to. Especially a duke like Ravensworth, who possessed a surety and seriousness that intimidated even Amelia.

Archie picked up the conversation. "I was just about to tell them about the night Ripon rescued that first-year."

"Rescued?" asked Amelia, despite her intention to show not a speck of curiosity about the blasted man.

Kilmuir snorted grumpily, and Ravensworth said, "That was his final year at Eton, no?"

Archie nodded. "He was two years—"

"Three," corrected Ravensworth.

"Three years above us. Anyway, this barmy little first-year got it into his head that he desperately missed his mummy and couldn't be away from her a minute longer."

"In the dead of night," said Ravensworth.

"In the middle of a freak snowstorm," said Kilmuir.

"Fortunately for the little bugger," continued Archie, "Ripon was returning from a late-night tea in the kitchens when he saw the lad escaping into the night wearing naught but his nightshirt, a wool scarf, and a pair of boots. Instead of sounding the alarm, he got dressed and retrieved the boy himself, though it took him several hours because the stupid lad got lost and stuck in a snowdrift."

"Both spent a few weeks with lung ailments, as I recall," said Ravensworth.

"But the prefect never found out," said Kilmuir.

"The head boy did."

"Oliver Quincy, wasn't it?"

"Ripon threatened to throttle him if he ever breathed a word."

"And Ripon didn't make idle threats."

"Anyone who ever met him on the rugby pitch knows it, too," said Kilmuir, unconsciously rubbing his shoulder.

"Like I said," said Archie, "a legend."

As if the mere mention of his name held the power to conjure the man, the Duke of Ripon appeared in the doorway. Amelia gasped and immediately felt embarrassed. Still, she only just caught herself before she started gawping. But, *oh*, the man did have a presence with his massive form and towering height and brooding glower that should render him brutish, but somehow came across as dangerously handsome.

"If it isn't the old chap himself," said Archie. "Come, have a seat and a bite."

Amelia avoided the table's greetings by asking a servant to set yet another place, this one directly across from her, for that was the seat Ripon chose.

How on earth was she expected to get through this night with that man sitting directly in her line of sight?

Fortunately, she wasn't expected to make conversation with him as Ravensworth began quizzing Ripon about his support for local building work, which led the conversation toward Ravensworth's own dedicated support for the arts in both Italy and England, which led to Ravensworth suggesting that Ripon take up a similar interest as he was an artist himself.

"A sculptor, no?" asked Ravensworth.

"Of sorts," said Ripon, as if the two words had been painfully extracted from him one by one.

The man wasn't the most sparkling supper conversationalist as his vocabulary seemed to consist of fewer than fifty words. Perhaps he was a brute.

Further, he kept staring at her. She could feel it. His attention made her uncomfortable, to be sure, but it sent another sensation fizzing through her as well—one she couldn't identify, but the one he always evoked.

It was as though her blood coursed hotter in her veins with a single cut of his stormy gray eyes.

As the lemon ice was being served, Juliet pushed away from the table. "That's me for the night. I think I'll see where Delilah skulked off to."

"Send her my regards," said Ravensworth.

Amelia's eyebrows lifted toward the ceiling—who knew Ravensworth could be saucy?—but Juliet remained cool. "I think I shan't."

Amelia could grudgingly admit she rather admired that quality about Juliet. She could tell off a duke without seeming to and simply walk away.

Archie dug his watch from a pocket. "If we're to make it to the Teatro della Pergola before the start of the first act, we must hop the twig."

Relief soared through Amelia. They would be leaving.

And by *they*, she meant one man—the ox.

But her relief wasn't to last long, for Archie asked, "Are you joining us, Ripon?"

What was this?

Impossibly, the duke shook his head. "I'm not much for evening entertainments."

Archie shrugged, and within thirty seconds, he was gone with Ravensworth and Kilmuir.

Which meant that within thirty seconds, Amelia was left alone with the Duke of Ripon.

How dare Archie invite Ripon to supper and not take the blasted man with him when he left? None of this would pass muster in London, that much she knew. Yet another reason she couldn't wait to return to her homeland and a sense of normality.

After the sweet course, but one course remained—cheese, usually her favorite. Tonight, it was like sand in her mouth. But she was determined to push through and send this man on his way in short fashion. Yet as she took one determined bite after another, she couldn't help noticing from the edge of her vision that the duke wasn't eating, or even drinking. Not a single bite or sip. Instead, he'd settled back in his chair and was staring at her.

What was he looking at, anyway? Had a large chunk of bleu cheese become lodged between her front teeth? A dribble of lemon ice down her bodice?

At last, she could take it no longer. A woman had her limits. "Why are you staring at me?"

"I'm a sculptor." He smiled. Or what passed for a smile with him. More of the suggestion of a smile. "And, very soon, you will be my subject. It's what I do."

"Well, you're making me..." Oh, she didn't want to finish that sentence. She suspected it would give him too much satisfaction.

He, however, decided to finish it for her. "*Uncomfortable?* Your cheeks do look flushed."

Amelia opened her mouth and closed it. He looked decidedly smug. She used her irritation as motivation and said, "You simply cannot speak that way to a young lady."

His mouth curled into the arrogant, condescending smile of a duke. "I can speak any way I like," he said. "Besides, you're not that young of a lady."

FOR SOME REASON that Tristan couldn't be bothered to explore, he enjoyed discomfiting the not-as-young-as-she-once-was Lady Amelia Windermere.

Just look at her—brow lifted to the ceiling…clear blue eyes round as saucers…pert mouth formed into a small, perfect O.

He'd shocked her speechless. A rare thing he would wager.

Delicately, she cleared her throat. "Perhaps you've been away from the niceties of proper society for too long, but one doesn't call attention to a lady's age whether she be young or not."

Tristan knew he should, but he felt not a bit chastened. Still, he conceded, "Fair enough." He hoped that would appease her, for he wouldn't be apologizing for speaking the plain truth.

Of course, she was beautiful—the *ton* would call her a diamond of the first water—that went without saying. Logic would follow that the only reason she was yet unmarried was through her own choice, not from a lack thereof.

Anyway, the subject bored him, and seeing as how they were the only two left at the table, conversation must be made. "So, what is it you do?" he asked, not particularly concerned with the answer.

Her brow knitted. "*Do?* Have you mistaken me for a washerwoman?"

He snorted. Why did aristocrats become so offended by the very notion of *doing* something? "You strike me as an industrious sort of woman, is all."

She pushed a piece of cheese around her plate with her fork and took to not looking at him, as if she could ignore him into nonexistence.

"What are your interests then?" he asked.

"I dabble in painting." Still, her gaze remained averted from him, now appearing to count the individual crystals in the chandelier above.

Her irritation was wearing off on him. "Dabble? You either paint or you don't," he all but growled.

Her gaze dropped to meet his. "I paint." The two simple words emerged prim, definite.

While he didn't have much use for the former adjective, the latter one intrigued. "Which medium?"

"Watercolors."

Tristan felt a frown forming on his mouth. He couldn't help feeling a little disappointed.

"Do you take issue with watercolors?" she asked, tapping her forefinger on the rim of her plate.

Since she was asking… "As a matter of fact, I do."

A laugh startled from her. "How can anyone find offense with watercolors? They are quite possibly the least offensive medium of any of the arts."

"That is precisely why they offend me. They make no statement. They don't dare me to feel."

She stared at him, head canted, flummoxed. He found that he liked flummoxing this woman more than he'd liked doing anything in months. Why not continue flummoxing her?

"Show me your watercolors."

Her mouth gave a wry twist. "They're but mere watercolors." There was no mistaking the sarcasm in her voice.

Of a sudden, his question meant to flummox turned into true desire. "I want to see them."

Her mouth perched on the edge of *no*. His ears fully expected it. Then her head canted to the other side, and different words spilled out. "Follow me."

She pushed away from the table and started walking without a backward glance. He shouldn't bite. He should march in the opposite direction and not stop until he was home. But she'd cast a lure, and he couldn't resist.

They entered a room, which he quickly realized was her bedroom. "This isn't an elaborate way of trapping me into marriage, is it?" The question was asked only half in jest. "I'm no great catch, I can assure you."

"Oh, I don't need your assurance to know that."

Her barb would sting if his skin weren't already thick as bison leather. Instead, he gave a dry laugh of appreciation.

She led him past the bed and sitting area to a studio space near double doors that opened onto a private terrace. On an easel sat a painting. Of a pomegranate. It was done well in terms of texture and color. No doubt she had a deft hand with a brush. But...

It did nothing for him.

She handed him another painting. A bowl of fruit. Then another bowl of fruit. The same fruit from the previous painting, in fact, but arranged in a different configuration. Then another...and another.

"What do you think?" she asked. She strove for nonchalance, but gave herself away with the twitchy glint in her eyes.

Tristan had never been skilled at disguising the truth. These watercolors were the bland work of a polite English lady. Which was disappointing. He'd thought there might be something impolite about this particular English lady.

"I had it in my mind that you would..." He stopped talking. He couldn't tell her what was in his mind. He'd thought her *more*.

Her eyes the blue of a particularly frigid glacier narrowed on him, and she seemed to make up her mind about something. In a few quick strides, she'd crossed the room to a bureau and began rifling through its top drawer. Seconds later, her hand emerged with a neat stack of watercolor papers.

More watercolors.

Tristan tried not to sigh too deeply, but *more watercolors*.

She returned and held the stack to her chest, uncertainty in her eyes. Curiosity sparked within Tristan, even as he couldn't help thinking how very beautiful Lady Amelia Windermere was in the moonlight streaming through the open double doors. Not the simple beauty of a young surface. *Deep-boned beauty*. The sort of beauty Botticelli would have immortalized in oil.

His hands were beginning to itch to sculpt her.

On a roughly exhaled sigh, she thrust the new stack of watercolors toward him. "These are...different."

He recognized the subject of the top painting. Dolce, Signore Rossi's dog, seated on his purple velvet pillow, poised for a round of barking by the look of it. Tristan couldn't help smiling as he flipped through the paintings. Scenes on various Florentine squares at different times of the day and sometimes night. Portraits of family members. Curious, those. None of her family were posed formally but, instead, depicted as they would be in life. Archer seated at a pianoforte. The cousin reading by a window. The sister clearly in the middle of one of her long-winded proclamations.

Tristan knew why in an instant. "Your family have no idea about these, do they?"

Lady Amelia bit her bottom lip between her teeth and shook her head. Nervousness shone in her eyes.

"They're good," he said. These paintings were better than good, but no need to get carried away. "Have you shown them to anyone?"

"I paint these for me."

"You've done something in a few brush strokes that painters dream and strive for their entire lives and few achieve."

"What is that?" she asked, cheeks flushed and eyes bright.

"You've captured the essence of the person or animal. I know them, just by looking at these paintings." He felt embarrassingly earnest.

Except he wasn't embarrassed, at all. No one should feel ashamed of their passion for art. It was the oxygen of a meaningful life, and did anyone feel embarrassed to have to draw breath?

Lady Amelia, for her part, stood three feet from him, blushing to the roots of her hair.

He would make her blush more before he was finished, for the longer he studied her paintings, the more he had to say about them. "It's a gift. *You* have a gift. You're a true artist."

Now her pulse was pounding so hard, he could see the rapid beats against the pale column of her neck. A few more words of praise and she just might reach climax, and how he would like to see that.

No.

Where had the thought come from?

Not from as remote a place in his mind as he would prefer.

He cleared his throat. "Have you considered oils?"

Her bearing shifted into the defensive. "Pardon?"

"With oils, you could considerably deepen all this."

She exhaled a dry, incredulous laugh. "They've made you feel something, haven't they?"

"They have." Now it was him on the defense.

"Then why shouldn't I continue to perfect the medium of my choice?"

Tristan didn't have a ready answer. She might be in the right. "You have connections in the arts. You could do a show."

"*Ladies* don't participate in art shows."

And like that, Tristan remembered who this woman was. A proper Englishwoman, bound by the rules of the aristocracy.

Yet these paintings hinted at a different woman.

He wasn't sure which woman he was trying to push with his next words, but he would speak them anyway because she needed to hear them. "There is really only one thing holding you back from becoming as great as you could be."

"And you know what this one thing is, I suppose." Her arms were crossed over her chest, and her jaw had a decidedly pugnacious set to it.

"I do."

"Enlighten me."

"You need to study the nude form."

Her mouth opened and closed and opened again.

She was about to give him an earful, surely. But what he wanted was for her to think about what he'd said, rather than simply react to it.

So, he did the only sensible thing. He handed the paintings back to her, gave a slight bow, pivoted on his heel, and exited the room through the open double doors, gone from the house in seconds and soon navigating the maze of Florentine streets beneath a clear, starry sky.

What had he been thinking in there? Speaking that way to a proper, unmarried English lady?

It mattered not.

He'd been following his instincts, and he'd been in the right.

Further, Lady Amelia Windermere was no simple proper English miss.

In fact, he sensed there may be something decidedly *improper* buried not so deep inside that particular English miss.

His logical side told him to leave it be—to leave *her* be. But his other side—the side that had brought him to Italy—knew he wouldn't be able to.

Chapter Five

Next day

A MELIA SQUIRMED ON the stool the servant had indicated and took in the space around her. Twenty-foot ceiling…walls of windows on three sides…busts, statues, and statuettes in various phases of completion in this corner…a spinning platform vast enough to hold an elephant in that corner. A bright, airy space with the breeze soughing through the cypress and olive trees outside. A view extending across the hills to the vast west. Perhaps if she squinted hard enough, she'd be able to make out the Mediterranean Sea.

She might be a speck envious of this studio.

A card emblazoned with a time and a street address had arrived alongside her cup of coffee this morning. She hadn't needed to ask to whom the address belonged.

The Duke of Ripon.

Today was to be her first sculpting session, and it would be his style to expect her simply to understand his intent. Arrogant, condescending man.

And—*oh*—that she'd known. That was the part that truly, deeply galled her.

He'd known that she would know.

And he'd known that she would be here.

Well, she hadn't arrived on time, a fact from which she took no small satisfaction. An hour late, in fact. He could stick that in his pipe and puff it.

Except now he seemed to be making her wait.

Which gave her time for reflection—the sort of time she most definitely didn't need.

She'd showed him her real art—her *true* art—the only art of genuine interest to her. The only other person who knew of it was Signore Rossi.

Then Ripon had had the nerve to mention *nudes*.

The absolute cheek of the man.

Didn't he know that ladies were meant only to paint for idle pleasure? Ladies didn't paint nude figures. To do so would only invite more scandal onto her family, and she'd had enough of that.

Except, perhaps his suggestion hadn't been cheek... Or not wholly cheek.

Perhaps it had been forthrightness. She might've detected as much in his eyes. A curiosity not bound by social niceties. It was maddening, yet...strangely enlivening, too—the not knowing what someone would say next.

Nudes, though...

A moderately young lady—she could concede she wasn't *young* young anymore—of marriageable age—at seven and twenty she hadn't quite reached the point of no return—painting people in the altogether? The very notion.

Yet he'd formed the notion and in the speaking of it had planted it squarely in her head.

To paint a living, breathing nude body, in all its shadow and light...flow and fluidity...places exposed...places hidden... She'd painted a number of the nude statues found on every square of Florence. Her studies of Michelangelo's *David* could fill volumes. No angle on that body remained unstudied by her keen eye. In fact, she'd scandalized a few fellow viewers one particular day with her acute concentration on his taut buttocks. While most of her observations flowed into her brush, others couldn't help wondering if a man's buttocks could possibly be *that* muscular and tight. She'd ended the day deciding it wasn't possible.

Movement caught the corner of her eye, and she turned. *Ripon*, striding through the doorway, all arrogant, condescending, masculine duke.

Except he didn't particularly look like a duke just now. He looked more similar to how she'd first encountered him. Like a man about to go build a stone wall with his bare hands.

The arrogance and condescension, however, that was all duke.

She opened her mouth to greet him, as was proper, but he strode straight past her without acknowledgement, only stopping at a table with a small, lumpy platform beside it, both draped with sheets.

"I must confess to a curiosity," she said.

He grunted and swept the sheets off the table and platform, revealing the tools of his art and a great unformed white lump of stone.

"How can you possibly expect to sculpt me without looking at me?"

He grunted again and picked up a hammer, then a chisel. She noticed the marble had already been roughly shaped. At last, he looked up at her.

She sucked in a deep breath, and her spine went straight as a ramrod. She wasn't sure how long she could keep up this position. What was clear, however, was that he wasn't meeting her eye. He was viewing her like an object. At last, he placed the chisel tip onto marble and made his first strike.

She jumped, then laughed sheepishly. She might've even detected the faint outline of a smile on the duke's face, but she couldn't be sure in the next second.

What a cacophonous business was sculpting. Such a lot of noise and labor to find the form in marble. But she could see he was striking with purpose and skill, not great blows, but careful placement of the chisel and banked strength behind the hammer strikes. It was both a brutal and delicate process, the rendering of his art.

Of a sudden, he stopped and laid down his instruments, the final strike of the hammer echoing through the studio.

What was he—

With a shrug of one great shoulder, then the other, he shed his coat. As he hadn't been wearing a cravat in the first place, but rather a simple red neckerchief, he now looked decidedly manly.

Like the most masculine man she'd ever beheld.

He rolled one sleeve, then the other, up to his elbows, and his manliness increased tenfold.

Heat suffused her body.

He picked up hammer and chisel again, and her gaze couldn't seem to remove itself from his forearms. A dusting of dark hair. Muscles both dense and sinewy, tensing and releasing beneath his skin, leading her gaze toward his hands. Massive, masculine hands. The hands of a brute. The hands of an artist, too. Those hands...

How would they feel upon flesh?

Her flesh.

It was only when he glanced up and met her eye that she realized she'd begun to fan herself. "Are you hot?"

Yes, she didn't say. *Perspiring buckets*, she didn't say either. "It's a bit close in here."

It wasn't. This light, airy studio was the perfect temperature.

It was her body that had taken on the heat of a hothouse in July.

"Remove your fichu."

A scandalized hand reached for her throat. "That's a rather forward request."

Ripon straightened, and his stormy gray gaze bored into her. "I need to see the line of your clavicle, and you're clearly burning up."

A familiar mulishness set in at the note of condescension in his voice. She pressed her lips together and didn't budge.

Ripon heaved a long-suffering sigh. "Can you put away the scandalized English miss for a bit?"

"Pardon?" she exclaimed, outraged.

"I've seen your paintings," he said. "I've seen who you really are. Or, at least, a glimpse of her."

Amelia's breath decided to stop. Could it be? That he saw...*her*?

Troubling, to be sure.

She'd opened a box of troubles last night, but she couldn't

quite bring herself to regret it. To be seen, fully seen, was a novel experience, and that it was this man of all people made her feel special. That he appreciated her work...

With a will of their own, her hands reached up and removed the fichu. It was only a scrap of lace, not her virtue, after all. A cooling breeze chose that moment to brush across her skin. Her eyes drifted shut in bliss. When they opened, they found his upon her, a look in his eyes she didn't recognize.

Her body seemed to. It seemed to want to melt beneath it, even as a feeling curled deep within her stomach, and deeper still to a place only she knew—and, quite honestly, not all that well.

Meanwhile, he kept working—placing chisel, striking chisel, cocking his head this way, then that, the crease in his brow growing ever deeper in the plain script of dissatisfaction. "Tilt your head slightly left," he said.

Amelia obeyed.

"I said *slightly*."

She overcompensated to the other direction, which only increased his grumpiness.

"*Slightly* lift your chin."

She lifted her chin.

"*Slightly*."

She exhaled a rough breath. "Are you a horse's arse to all your models?"

His eyebrows drew together. "I'm giving you direction."

Amelia snorted for perhaps the first time in her life. It was a surprisingly freeing experience.

He started up on the marble again, but his dissatisfaction only increased until he set his tools down on an abrupt clatter and made for her. Alarm streaked through her. What was he—

Then he was standing squarely before her, not a foot away, staring intently, seeing her and yet somehow not seeing her in the objective way an artist viewed his subject. And there was his scent again—clove, sandalwood, and sweat.

She cleared her throat and opened her mouth to speak when he did it: he laid his large hands upon her shoulders and cleared all rational thought from her brain. His hands were warm, almost hot, his heat seeping into her with every rapid beat of her heart. Strong, too, their latent strength apparent. They could crush her if they chose, but they were gentle, one remaining on her shoulder and the other tucking beneath her chin, nudging it up by small increments, his intense gaze upon her...

It was only when he said, *"There,"* that she realized her eyes had drifted shut.

"Stay exactly as you are," he said, the words a deep, velvet rumble across his throat.

An involuntary quiver shimmered through her.

Back at the marble, he chiseled for a few more minutes before his frown of frustration returned. Then he was again standing before her, sharing her air, touching her—squaring her shoulders, relaxing her shoulders, tipping her chin up, then down, nudging the back of her head to push it forward to... She wasn't sure what precisely he was seeking to accomplish. All she could do was breathe him in and struggle against improper thoughts about his hands and the muscles rippling along his forearms. The heat of him... The manliness of him... She'd never been in the presence of such a masculine being, much less had his hands upon her...

For her own peace of mind, she cleared her throat. He glanced down and blinked.

And she knew. He was now *seeing* her, not as a model to be molded like clay, but *her*.

The air between them went still and intimate. The sky could've crashed down about their heads, and Amelia wouldn't have noticed for, *here*, in this instant of time something in her recognized something in him.

Her mouth parted, and her desire, sudden and deep, spilled out of her. "I want to paint you."

"Oh?" He didn't seem too intrigued.

"Nude."

He went still as stone. "I cannot have heard you correctly."

The boldness that had pushed her desire from her mouth didn't relent. "Shall I repeat myself?"

He gave his head a bemused shake, breaking the moment. He pivoted and returned to his hammer and chisel. He wasn't taking her seriously.

She could stamp her foot with frustration, but that would only reinforce his assessment that she was spoilt and didn't know her own mind, like a child. So, she sat and steamed and stewed in her humiliation as it settled in that she'd propositioned a duke—*a duke!*—to strip nude for her. The sultry Italian air must've been having an effect.

"And *I* want to sculpt *you*," he said. "But we don't always get what we want, do we?"

What an odd thing for him to say. "You *are* sculpting me."

He shrugged, and his eyes narrowed on the marble before him. "All of you."

"All of me?"

Oh.

"*All* of me."

"But that isn't done with members of polite society."

Polite. Never in her life had she taken issue with the word polite.

Never before now.

Further, she didn't particularly care for the way he was throwing that word at her. Hadn't she just been impolite?

She should storm off in a huff, but it struck her that she'd started this impolite conversation and every fiber in her being wanted to follow where it led.

"How much is *all* of me?" she asked.

His gray gaze caught hers and held it. "Every line. Every curve. Every inch."

Oh, she felt hot...so *hot*. And her breath. It'd caught in her throat. "I can't imagine my lines and curves are all that different from any other woman's lines and curves."

"My imagination is telling me otherwise."

His imagination...

He'd been imagining her...

Her lines and curves...

Every inch of her body.

The very blood in her veins coursed hot, and her skin felt...*excitable*. As if one touch from him would cause an explosion.

He was ten feet away, and yet he made her feel so...

"You want to sculpt me"—the next word had trouble escaping her mouth—"*nude*."

"Yes."

No longer did his manner convey disinterest or nonchalance. He'd gone completely and utterly intense. Still, she detected a glimmer of distance, of distrust. He didn't think for an instant that she would agree. He thought he had her. Maybe he did, because how could she...

Except...

How badly did she want it? How badly did she want to defy his expectations of her?

Until she'd met this man, she'd never thought anything wrong with her desire to conform to society's rules and expectations. But this duke...

She wanted to defy him.

And confound him.

He thought he had her measure. Well...

"You have a bargain."

His knowing smile fell, then froze. *She* had flummoxed *him*. No small victory, that.

"Pardon?"

"You heard me."

"And, to be clear, the bargain is that if I pose nude for you, you shall pose nude for me."

"Yes."

It occurred to Amelia that she could be a different sort of person with this man. Someone who veered closer to the heart of who she truly was. Someone society had never seen. Even her siblings didn't know this Amelia.

The look in his eyes shifted, no longer distant, but considering. "I'll get what I want, and you'll get what you need."

"And what is it I need?" she asked, a bit breathless.

"Experience," he said, his gaze unrelenting. "And I can give it to you with my body."

Yet another blade of heat struck through Amelia, and for a

moment she forgot what they were even discussing.

"You need to fully immerse yourself in the human form to deepen your work."

Were they still talking about painting? Because her body and that secret place *down there* seemed to have a very different idea—*and hope*—that he was talking about something else.

He closed the distance between them and extended his hand. "You have a deal."

She hesitated for the briefest moment, panic threatening to overtake her. She allowed it no air as she placed her hand in his. The contact lasted but a few seconds, but she felt the imprint of his skin scorch upon hers.

A fire lit silver within his eyes. A determination, too.

Anticipation slid up Amelia's spine, curled in her gut... and lower too. Anticipation of what, she wasn't certain. But she did know she'd never felt more alive in her seven and twenty years than she did in this instant.

She reclaimed her hand and wobbled ungracefully to her feet. She needed to get away from this man, so she could *think*. "I'll, um, see you...soon."

And her boot heels were clicking against the terracotta tiled floor, and she was exiting through the exterior door, upsetting the peace of his inner courtyard in her mad scramble to be away.

Surely, he watched her through the window.

And, surely, he expected her to go back on their agreement.

In truth, she half expected it, too. Except...

She had something to learn from that man. She wasn't sure what it was, but she knew one thing.

Only he could teach her.

Chapter Six

Next evening

A MELIA HAD NEVER encountered Signore Rossi's villa by night. With warm lantern light casting lively shadows against mellow stone walls and sparkling fountains and the scent of lemon and fig drifting on the air, this courtyard would have been enchanting if not for the obvious: all the other people. Dressed in their evening finery, they milled about, crystal coupes in their hands, ready laughter on their mouths.

Just inside the gate—one foot out, really—Amelia stood observing the scene, feeling like nothing more than a fish out of water. She'd considered politely refusing Signore's invitation, as she had all others these last few months, having assumed it would be a bohemian sort of crowd that would do her and her family's reputation no favors.

And as her gaze swept the courtyard, she suspected she'd been correct. She hadn't even been announced. To be sure, she'd received no few curious glances, but no one appeared particularly bothered by the presence of an unmarried, unaccompanied lady.

A server stopped before her, his arm laden with a silver tray topped with at least ten coupes effervescing with prosecco. It was clear she was to take one. Which she did. She didn't have to drink it.

Well, maybe just a sip.

Fizzy and sweet, the prosecco danced on her tongue.

Delightful.

Another sip of prosecco loosed an honest thought. The reason she was here tonight after refusing Signore's other invitations. The possibility existed that *he* might be here. After all, this was where she'd first encountered him. And after their bargain, she couldn't seem to rid her mind of the dratted man. She'd even dreamt of him last night.

Oh, the dream…

She couldn't think about the dream.

Yet parts of her, dark and private, couldn't seem to stop.

She took a long, long sip of prosecco. Somehow, a fresh coupe had found its way into her hand. It helped push the thought away.

Somewhat.

As if her dream had turned into substance, Ripon appeared across the courtyard, on the other side of the nymph fountain. Her eyes hadn't the will to leave him be. Dressed in evening blacks, he was just so very handsome. Her gaze followed the width of his broad shoulders down the length of arms nearly too muscular for his evening coat to his hands. Those hands looked slightly ridiculous holding a delicate prosecco coupe.

She might feel jealous of that coupe.

Yet something about him looked different tonight. Then she realized what it was: he wasn't wearing his customary scowl. Perhaps even the hint of a curve hovered about his mouth, which was as close to a smile as she'd ever seen on him.

Her fingers itched for a paintbrush. A few strokes would capture him as he was now.

His eye began to wander away from his companions, slowly making its way toward… *her*. Her heart kicked against her ribs. Her breath went short and sharp. His gaze brushed across her and the breath stopped in her lungs as they stood fifty feet apart, unable to release their gazes from one another.

Then it happened.

His mouth turned downward.

The scowl had returned.

A stray giggle wanted to bubble up. She took a sip of prosecco to stifle it.

The scowl deepened.

Which only summoned another giggle.

The prosecco might be stifling the giggles, but the possibility existed it might be provoking them, too.

"*Mi scusi, signorina*," came a husky feminine voice to her left.

Somehow, Amelia dragged her eyes away from the duke and found a woman draped in strand upon strand of pink pearls staring at her expectantly. "*Si?*"

"Are you the sister of the Viscount Archer?"

Amelia gave the woman a subtle once-over. Lush and beautiful and clearly either married or widowed, she was precisely the sort of woman with whom Archie would acquaint himself. "I am Lady Amelia Windermere," she said.

The woman smiled at the group forming a semicircle around them. "See? I told you she must be."

Amelia found herself unwillingly drawn into conversation as the striking similarity between the Windermere siblings was discussed—tall, striking, and very blonde—which evolved into a more general discussion about siblings and their similarities and dissimilarities.

Amelia went for another sip of prosecco and found her coupe empty. Serendipitously, at that very moment, a sparkling silver tray appeared before her.

As the conversation began to exhaust itself, Signore Rossi jumped into the breach. "Signorina Amelia *es una cima* with the watercolor brush. I hope she will allow her work to be shown before she returns to England."

Interest entered a few sets of eyes, and pride stole through Amelia. She'd never received such praise in the public sphere. She might like it.

Something else she liked: how she felt from her fingertips to her toes. She'd never felt this good in her life. Why had no one ever told her about prosecco? How had she made it to the age of seven and twenty without knowing its magic?

With a renewed confidence, and another few sips of prosecco, she turned toward the lady to her right—a new one had appeared—and asked, "And when are you expecting?" In England, she would never ask such a question in mixed company, but in

Italy, such rules didn't seem to apply.

"Expecting what, *mia cara?*" the lady asked with a puzzled smile.

"Your baby."

Puzzlement turned into utter confusion. Perhaps her English wasn't fluent.

"I only ask," continued Amelia, "because a dear friend of mine who married before me—actually all my dear friends have married before me." She dismissed the wave of self-pity that tried to surge. "Anyway, when she was about your size, she got a case of the hiccups that lasted for an entire fortnight."

The woman blinked, her brow deeply furrowed.

"You'll never guess the remedy."

The woman continued staring at Amelia. Or was she glaring?

"Fresh sardines," said Amelia. "One bite, and the hiccups were gone. The only problem was that she ate sardines for the remainder of her confinement. One could hardly stand to be in a room with her." She waved a hand in front of her face. "The breath."

A solid five seconds beat by before the lady emitted a spew of rapid Italian into Amelia's face. Once finished, the lady charged away.

Amelia remained unperturbed, even sympathetic. "Expecting ladies can be quite temperamental. All my friends were."

Signore Rossi cleared his throat. "Signora Fontana is not with child."

"Oh, dear," said Amelia, "should I go and—"

A hand wrapped around her upper arm. A large, calloused, strong hand. She glanced up and found the Duke of Ripon staring down at her, his opaque gray eyes giving nothing away. "You've done enough."

Signore Rossi redirected the subject with the fluidity of a skilled host, and the stream of conversation began to flow around Amelia and Ripon. Awareness of him—of his body only inches from hers—raced along her skin, lighting her veins as it skittered through. His hand had fallen away, but she could still feel the outline of his fingers on her skin.

By chance, her gaze landed on the older, bespectacled German gentleman across from her. Something about his ear... She squinted. A small, furry animal of some sort—a caterpillar?—appeared to be nesting there. She couldn't decide if it was repulsive or cute.

As discreetly as possible, she gave a little wave and waggle of her fingers in his direction.

"What are you doing?" Ripon hissed into her ear.

"Trying to get the *herr*'s attention."

"Whatever for?" He sounded no small bit suspicious.

Before she could answer, she succeeded in securing the herr's attention, even as she was all too aware of Ripon at her side. "Pardon me, *herr*, but I have a question for you."

"Oh?" the man asked, strangely wary.

"Is the small, furry animal in your ear a pet?"

The herr turned a particular shade of purple that couldn't be good for his health. "*Fräulein*, who are you to go around a civilized gathering, hurling insults at everyone you lay eyes upon?"

Again, the hand wrapped around her upper arm. This time it tugged.

"That's quite enough for tonight."

⚸

AS TRISTAN GUIDED Lady Amelia across the courtyard, through Signore Rossi's open villa, and onto the quiet terrace at the back of the house, it occurred to him that he didn't have the right.

After all, he wasn't her brother or husband or even fiancé.

Or lover.

Definitely not that.

But he wasn't doing it for her. He was doing it for everyone else. A Lady Amelia Windermere with a few drinks in her was a menace to society.

She jerked to a stop, outraged eyes rounding on him. "Who do you think you are? King of the villa?"

"A duke."

"Yes, well, hyperbole." She rolled her eyes toward the sky. "I know you're a duke. Everyone knows, don't they?"

"Everyone seems to."

"And you don't like that, do you?"

What Tristan didn't like was how Lady Amelia had turned the conversation around on him.

Or how she was looking at him.

As if she could see into him.

That wouldn't do. He needed to get her out of here. The woman was completely foxed.

"If we follow the path around the villa to the alleyway," he said, "I can summon my coachman to drive you to your villa."

Her brow furrowed. "To my villa? Why would I go there?"

"Because you've managed to insult every person you've spoken to tonight?"

Her head tipped back, and a smile broadened across her face. "But look at the moon."

He didn't need to. He was looking at its goddess, her hair shining silver in the light, her eyes the clear blue of an East Indian sea. Her beauty was nearly too much to gaze upon, as if the moon would exact a price from those who stared too long.

Possibly at the direction of her mistress, Lady Amelia backed one step away from him, then another, mischief in her eyes. Then she whirled around and vanished into Rossi's garden. Tristan had no choice but to follow.

Ahead, an object shone white on the ground. He grabbed it and held it to the moonlight. A flimsy scrap of lace. A lady's fichu, if he wasn't mistaken. Lady Amelia had been wearing a fichu.

"Lady Amelia," he called out, muted so her name wouldn't carry to the villa.

A faint *yes* sounded in the distance.

"Have you lost something?" Like her inhibitions, for starters.

Another sound floated across the still night air. Was that a giggle?

"Oh, I would say a few somethings."

What on earth—

He rounded a bend of high shrubbery and beheld what on

earth, indeed.

A fountain.

Lady Amelia.

Lady Amelia splashing in the fountain, wearing nothing but stays, stockings, and a chemise.

Playful...wet...

His cock sprang to instant life.

"Oh, it feels so good," she cooed. "The water and the breeze against one's bare skin. I've never felt so...*good.*"

Oh, he—and his cock—could think of a few ways to make her feel even better than good.

He cleared his throat. "You must come out of there at once," he commanded with all the ducal authority he could muster. Which was a great deal, even under the current circumstances.

She acted as if she hadn't heard him and began floating on her back.

Little of her was left to the imagination.

She was as exquisite as his imagination had insisted—long, slender, yet all the lines of her so very feminine.

"*Out,*" he barked.

"I think not." She hadn't even bothered to look at him.

Tristan wasn't accustomed to people ignoring his commands. It irked him. Especially when any rational person could see he was in the right.

Of course, Lady Amelia was no longer a rational person. She was a person stewed to the gills.

He moved to the edge of the fountain. "*Now.*"

"I'm afraid not."

"Don't make me come in after you."

"You won't."

She spoke the last bit with a certainty that rubbed against his last remaining nerve.

That was it.

With focused efficiency, he shed coat, waistcoat, and cravat, stripped down to shirt and trousers. That was as far as he would go. What if someone happened upon them, and he was in the buff?

He would have to marry the chit.

That was what.

Even in Italy.

"How fussy you are," she said, blithe and unconcerned.

On a great charge, he cleared the lip of the fountain and sank to his waist in an instant.

"It's deeper than you'd think," she said with the wisdom of one who had gone before.

That irked him, too.

In five great strides, the water dragging against him, he reached her. For her part, she remained floating on her back, staring up at him, small nipples hard as cherry pits through the translucent muslin of her chemise.

Now what?

What the bloody hell had he been thinking? Did he mean to lay hands on her?

That would be a bad idea.

A very, very bad idea.

"You wouldn't dare touch me," she said, and laughed with all the unconcern of the innocent.

He remained silent, unable to trust himself to speak. He wouldn't *dare*?

"Your reputation is so very salacious, but I've found little to warrant it. Surprising, really." She scoffed. "The Dissolute Duke, my arse."

What was this? Was he some flaccid, toothless old man?

Well, wasn't she in for a surprise?

In another great stride, he closed the remaining distance between them, taking particular delight in watching her uncon-cerned smile transform into very concerned shock as she bolted upright and began a sloshy scramble away from him.

But she'd started too late.

He was scooping her up in the next instant. Of their own accord, her arms lifted and slid around his neck to steady herself. Her face separated from his by mere inches, they stared at each other in utter shock. Her arms began to tighten around his neck and her lips parted a fraction, wide enough for her tongue to dart out and wet them. Before he understood what she was about, her mouth was pressed against his.

A wave of impressions flooded him. *Soft...sweet...* She tasted of sugar...of prosecco and lemon and woman...of everything delicious in the world.

On carnal instinct, his tongue slid through her parted lips, unable to resist a deeper taste of her, knowing to his bones a taste would never be enough...

She gasped.

And like that, he knew what else she tasted of.

Innocence.

He jerked back, tearing himself away from the kiss, and met eyes wide with shock. He didn't kiss innocent women. Further, he didn't kiss tippled women, especially when he was stone sober. And this woman wasn't just any woman, but an unmarried one. Most assuredly a virgin, her reaction to his tongue told her.

Right.

Confusion and curiosity warring in her eyes, her arms tightened around his neck, bringing her mouth closer to his. The chit was trying to kiss him...*again.*

He averted his face and began wading to the edge of the fountain. For such a tall woman, she weighed hardly anything, even sopping wet. He nearly dropped her when her mouth found his neck, her warm breath raising goose bumps along his skin.

Then she licked him, her tongue a slick drag up his neck.

Was the woman trying to get herself ravished?

"Mm, salty," she said, breathy. "I wonder where else you're salty."

He could provide a thorough tutorial.

Stoically, he kept moving until they reached the grass, where he unceremoniously deposited her. "Dress yourself," he commanded and pivoted so his back faced her. He couldn't watch her struggle into her clothes, without offering to help.

Perhaps not without helping himself to *her.*

And that would be ungentlemanly.

While he'd come to Italy to *not* be a gentleman, a man must adhere to a few principles. Not taking advantage of an intoxicated woman was one of them.

But, oh, how his body screamed for just one more taste of her...

A throat cleared behind him. He turned to find she'd dressed herself...somewhat. Her hair was half up and half down, and thoroughly sodden, and her dress might be on backwards, but it was enough to preserve her modesty from prying eyes.

His prying eyes, to be exact.

Side by side, they followed the path that led around the side of the villa.

"About our bargain," she said.

Perhaps she'd come to her senses and thought better of it.

"Yes?"

"I'll expect you at my villa tomorrow night—" Her brow furrowed. "Tonight?"

He nodded. It had grown late.

"For our first painting session."

"You cannot be serious."

"And bring a fig leaf."

"A fig leaf?"

"To preserve your modesty."

For the first time in what felt like an age of thirty years— perhaps it had been—he laughed, long and hard and without reserve. It cleansed, this sort of laughter. But, really, the things that emerged from this woman's mouth. "You mean to preserve *your* modesty," he said.

"Whatever do you mean?"

"You'll see."

Could she truly be that innocent?

He looked into her eyes.

She could.

"Midnight," she continued. "You know where my bedroom is located."

They reached the alleyway, but before they emerged from the shadows, he signaled that she stop. "Stay put and out of sight."

With a sharp whistle, he caught his driver's attention. Within a few minutes, the carriage rolled into view. Tristan waved it as close as could be managed. Even so, Lady Amelia would be exposed to a good five feet of light. The unconcerned eye would find nothing amiss. The gossipy eye, however...

She was a Windermere. That was what people would say. What they didn't understand about Lady Amelia, however, was that she was a different sort of Windermere.

He opened the carriage door and waved at her. She seemed to understand the mission, for she dashed as fast as her sloshy slippers could carry her and made a mad scramble inside the carriage *tout suite*. As she passed him, he might've even caught a few droplets of spray from her hair, which now streamed down her back in wet blonde streaks.

Once inside, she stared straight ahead and didn't acknowledge his existence. She might've sobered up a bit.

He poked his head into the open window. "One bit of advice," he said to the side of her face. "When you get home, drink a large glass of water. Your morning self will thank you."

He pulled back and gave the side of the carriage two sharp raps.

As he watched the carriage speed off into the night, he knew what he should do. He should send a note first thing tomorrow backing out of their bargain.

But he wouldn't.

He knew that, too.

Chapter Seven

Next evening

A S TRISTAN HAD known he would, he'd come.
And here he stood in her garden, beyond the terrace,
beyond the edge of light.

He'd been standing like this for a full ten minutes.

Staring…

At Lady Amelia, illuminated by the warm, yellow glow of the
two candelabras in her studio, as she moved carefully and
seriously, readying her materials for his arrival—easel placed
before a straight-backed chair, indicating she would sit while she
painted; brushes arranged with meticulous care at precise
intervals on a small table; paints and water ready to be mixed and
made into magic on paper.

He shouldn't be here, he understood that. But he was an
adult and, last night's escapade in Rossi's fountain notwithstand-
ing, she was an adult, too. And as adults they'd made a bargain.
Further, he was a gentleman; he wouldn't be breaking his oath.

But…as a gentleman, shouldn't he?

Well, he was here, so that was *that* decided.

Except he was watching her through her open double doors
like a lecher.

Right.

He cleared his throat, and her head whipped around, her clear
blue gaze searching the night beyond the terrace for him. He had
no choice but to step into the light. She didn't smile or greet him
in any way, but simply kept arranging brushes that had already

been resituated three times since he'd arrived, and however many more before that. She was nervous.

He entered the studio and decided it would be best to get the obvious out of the way. "About last night," he began.

Bent over the small table, she froze. Very deliberately, she straightened her long, elegant body, squared her shoulders, and faced him. "I licked your neck."

His eyebrows lifted toward the ceiling. They couldn't help themselves. That was certainly the obvious sorted.

"And...and..." she continued, her cheeks and the tips of her ears glowing pink. "And I apologize." She swallowed. "Profound-ly."

Tristan hadn't known what to expect, but it wasn't this. A *profound* apology. He didn't want her apology, profound or not. What he wanted, if he was being truthful, was for her to lick his neck again. He'd detected some talent in that tongue of hers.

But he wouldn't say that. Any of it. Instead, he picked up the sound of piano drifting on the air. "Is that music coming from this villa?"

"Oh, that's Archie."

"Archie? Your brother?"

A tiny smile formed about her mouth. "There's only one Archie, Your Grace."

Intricate and skilled, the music carried on, each note following the next with inevitability. *Nay.* Archie wasn't simply *skilled.* "He plays magnificently." An idea about the Windermere siblings occurred to him. "And Lady Delilah, does she have artistic ability?"

"This may come as an utter shock," said Lady Amelia, dry as dust, "but she's an actress, by desire if not by trade."

"And your cousin?" He might as well ask. "Has she an artistic skill?"

"Juliet rather keeps herself to herself, but she does scribble an awful lot in her notebooks."

"A writer then."

"I've been on the lookout for an anonymously published serial about a trio of scandalous siblings," said Lady Amelia, her tone still wry, but a twinkle in her eye.

Tristan snorted. Lady Amelia could be entirely too serious. He liked that she could be funny, too. "You Windermeres have hidden depths."

She swallowed and cleared her throat, all traces of humor falling away. Her nervous gaze flicked toward the settee. The air seemed to change its elemental composition in an instant. "If you will have a seat"—she inhaled a tiny sip of air—"we can begin."

Taking his sweet time, Tristan lowered himself onto saffron velvet and spread his legs wide, taking up three quarters of the surface area. She would have to move closer to him to take her place at the easel, which would leave her four or so feet from him. Now that he'd assumed his place, she would be realizing that four feet was nothing. Actually, in this room, at this hour, only the two of them, it was *something*. It was a distance that flirted on the edge of intimacy. An amount of space easily surmounted to achieve it. Awareness of what could be tremored through his body.

Without venturing closer than absolutely necessary, she slipped into her chair and dipped a brush into the water dish, stirring it into a pot of paint, then repeating the process. She appeared to be working her way up to asking him a question.

And he knew exactly which question that would be. "Would you like me to remove my coat?"

She met his gaze around her easel. "If you would," she croaked.

He shrugged the garment off his shoulders and tossed it aside. "Perhaps my waistcoat, too?" he asked, the very soul of politeness.

"Yes, please."

"And my cravat?"

All out of words, she bit her bottom lip between her teeth and nodded. Perhaps it was ungentlemanly, but this was fun. He rather liked making Lady Amelia Windermere go speechless. Slowly, deliberately, he unknotted his cravat, giving her gaze no choice but to watch. His shirt fell open into a wide V, revealing his dark fuzz of chest hair, and he settled back. "Anything else?"

"Um, that's all for the moment." A beat. "Thank you."

Without asking, he rolled his shirt sleeves to his elbows. She watched every movement from start to finish. And after he'd done, there her gaze remained. Her eyes had gone nearly black with the flare of her pupils, the blue of her irises a thin ring. Interesting.

She picked up a nub of charcoal and began sketching, her gaze flicking back and forth between the easel and his forearms, suddenly an artist in her element. Her demeanor began to relax as she settled into her flow. He liked her this way—at ease with him, treating him as her subject.

But here was the thing: he wasn't simply her subject, like a bowl of fruit, no matter how she might will the idea into reality. He was very much a man—one whose lips she'd kissed, whose neck she'd licked. "You needn't have apologized," he said.

Her brush stopped. "I took advantage of you."

A laugh burst from him. No conversation was ever predictable with this woman. "That's a first."

"And your gallantry," she said. Her head canted, and she looked at him. Really looked at him. "Which does beg a question."

"Oh?" He might want to brace himself.

"I can't quite square this gallantry of yours with your big bad scandalous reputation," she said. "How did you come by it? Were you genuinely so rotten to your fiancée?"

"Yes." It was simply true. But he could see from the curiosity in her eyes that he wouldn't be getting away with the simple answer. And for some strange reason, he felt like giving this woman the long answer he'd never given anyone. "I became a duke at the grand old age of three years."

"Your father died young."

He nodded. "In a boating accident."

"That must've been devastating for your mother."

Lady Amelia's empathy caught Tristan on the back foot. "He was the love of her life, and she never quite recovered."

"She didn't remarry?"

He shook his head. He could tell Lady Amelia more. That

he'd learned a valuable lesson from his mother. If one never gave oneself over to great love, one never left oneself vulnerable to great loss. The sort of loss that never let up or let go.

But that wasn't the conversation they were having, so he wouldn't. "From then on, essentially," he continued, "I did everything I was supposed to do and embodied everyone I was supposed to be—good son to my mother, good student at Eton and Cambridge, good duke to my lands and tenants. Then the day arrived that it was decided I was to be a good husband."

"An achievable goal, surely."

He snorted. *If only.* "It so happened that father's bosom friend had a daughter of marriageable age. I allowed my mother to arrange the match."

"It sounds so very cold."

Tristan shrugged. "From my experience, one young lady is about the same as any other. They must drink the same water to turn themselves into bland, agreeable ciphers."

Lady Amelia's face twisted with instant outrage. "Oh, spoken just like a man," she exclaimed.

Her vehemence took him aback. He hadn't said anything anyone didn't know—particularly the young ladies themselves, surely. "Pardon?"

"Do you not have any idea what girls and young ladies are put through to secure their futures? Have you never considered that bland agreeableness is a mask we are schooled to use? Our futures depend upon it as it seems the male sex simply cannot accept our true selves," she finished in a huff.

He let her words blow over him before conceding. "Fair enough."

Her jaw unclenched. But she wasn't done. "Tell me more about this fiancée."

"There isn't much to tell about Lady Sarah."

"That simply cannot be true."

"Oh, but it is."

She laughed, no humor in it. "I see now."

"You do?" he asked slowly. He sensed no good could come from that.

"You see marriage as women's business."

"Isn't it?"

"Has it never occurred to you that two are in a marriage."

"Not particularly." From what he could tell, women had the running of the wedded state. But he would keep that opinion to himself. Lady Amelia's glare wasn't having it.

"Why did Lady Sarah jilt you?"

Whatever his answer, Tristan understood he would be found at fault. But he stood on firm ground here. "If you must know—"

"I must." Lady Amelia was clearly determined.

"It was she who asked me an imprudent question."

"Which was?" she asked, suspicious.

"She asked if I loved her."

"And your reply?"

"I, well…" It occurred to him that his answer might not reflect well on him. "I snorted."

"You snorted?" Lady Amelia's gaze narrowed. "What else?"

"I told her I'd only met her twice."

"And she said?"

He shifted uncomfortably. The ground was less firm here. "She pointed out that we, in fact, had met eight times."

"She'd been counting."

"But, really," he began. If he didn't come to his own defense, who would? "How is meeting a person on eight occasions enough time to love them?"

Lady Amelia simply sat regarding him as if his head had become screwed on backwards. "There's more."

Tristan saw no way out of this conversation but through. "Lady Sarah asked if I ever could."

"And you said?"

"No."

"And she said?"

"'A woman needs to be adored every now and again.'" He spread his hands wide in a gesture of helplessness. "I politely informed her that wouldn't be possible."

"You told your fiancée—the woman you were to spend the rest of your life with—that you would never adore her?"

"Or any other woman, to be fair." He shrugged. "It was only the truth."

Lady Amelia's brow furrowed. "But why deny yourself?"

"I deny myself nothing," he said. "Just ask the gossips."

"Oh, but you do," she said. "It's the most wonderful feeling in the world to adore something or someone, to feel absolutely smitten. Sometimes it's a beloved pet or a particularly juicy peach or a new dress—"

"I'll have to take your word for that one."

She wasn't to be interrupted. "But the feeling fills you as if you're bursting with light. To adore feels better than to be adored, and yet you deny yourself the feeling."

"Perhaps I don't have the same capacity as you."

Lady Amelia shook her head. "I've seen you at your work, your passion for it. That's adoration. You have the capacity." Her head canted. "And that's why Lady Sarah jilted you?"

"In part."

"You're about to tell me what set off the scandal, aren't you?"

"I merely informed her—politely, as one adult to another— that was what lovers were for."

Lady Amelia's mouth gaped. He'd shocked her. It was, as a matter of fact, the same expression Lady Sarah's face had taken.

"It's true then," said Lady Amelia, aghast. "You told her to take lovers."

Tristan shifted uncomfortably. "A suggestion, really. She wasn't obliged to take me up on it."

"You...you...you..." sputtered Lady Amelia. Tristan couldn't decide if she was lost for words or had too many clamoring to get out. "You are a singularly infuriating man."

He shrugged. "And that was the last I ever saw of Lady Sarah Locksley."

"But not heard of her."

"The gossip does have a habit of haunting my footsteps."

Lady Amelia tapped paintbrush to mouth. "What I don't follow is how you went from there to Italy. You're a duke and, really, it's not an unsurvivable scandal for a duke."

He sensed a raw spot in her words. "And you would know all

about that?"

"I'm acquainted with the subject."

He didn't have to tell her the next part, but for some reason he wanted to. "It was through my mother's grace and understanding. She understood that I needed a taste of freedom. A taste of life outside the structure and inflexibility of being a duke. So, she came to me with an offer. She would give me five years of freedom. She'd run the estates during my minority, and she'd do it again."

"She offered you the opportunity to experience life as a man, not a duke," said Lady Amelia. He detected understanding in her words, in her eyes.

"At the end of those five years, I would return and resume my duty."

"How old were you?"

"Thirty."

"And what age are you now?"

"Four and thirty."

"You have one more year."

"Six months." *Not even.*

"You don't want to return to England." It wasn't a question, but a statement of fact.

"Would you?"

"I do."

Intimacy pulsed between them. Not the sort of intimacy his body wanted from her, but that of the intangible. An intimacy he couldn't remember experiencing with anyone else. Two instincts warred inside him—to draw in...to pull back. He could ask her why she wanted to return to England so badly and learn more about her, or he could leave it.

The simple fact was he didn't need to know *why*, or anything else about Lady Amelia Windermere. It was better if he didn't. She was already haunting his dreams and turning him into the sort of lech who watched women from outside their windows. Better this bargain was fulfilled and behind them.

"Aren't you going to ask me to remove my shirt?" he asked.

Like a man who had just lobbed a grenade, he sat back and

waited for it to explode.

In an instant, she went tense, and he detected a slight tremble in the hairs of her paintbrush. "Of course." She swallowed as if her throat had gone suddenly dry. "Will you remove your shirt?"

With deliberate ease, he slipped the garment over his head. When he opened his eyes, he caught her in the act of staring at him—her gaze roving across his bare chest, drinking in the sight of him. He'd never had virgin eyes laid upon him. He felt strangely exposed. What was that flare in her eyes? *Desire?*

He cleared his throat, and she startled. Stirred into action, she dipped her brush in water and began to pull the fine tip against paper. It was as if he could feel those brush strokes against his skin.

Though phantom, it was quite possibly the most sensual feeling he'd ever almost experienced.

"Do you need me to move?" he asked, feeling as if he needed to say something.

She gave her head a curt shake, entirely immersed in her work.

Surprise ribboned alongside awareness through his body. He hadn't at all anticipated the intimacy of this experience.

And Lady Amelia... She was sensual—her skill...her focus...everything about her. Before him was the Lady Amelia no one else had ever glimpsed.

He wanted her.

It occurred to him he might sacrifice anything to have her.

"Shall I remove my trousers?" he asked, the question gravel in his throat.

Her gaze flew up to meet his, the brush in her hand gone still, the breath caught in her chest.

"But I must warn you."

"Of?" she asked, breathless.

"I forgot my fig leaf at home."

Horror turned into amusement, and she laughed. A relief, that laugh. He thought she would run screaming from her own bedroom. But perhaps Lady Amelia Windermere was made from sterner stuff.

"Um, yes." She reached for a glass and took a large gulp of water. "You may remove your trousers."

Tristan stood, and she shifted away, presenting him with the cold of her shoulder and the side of her face as she began fiddling with her paint palette and brushes. There was no mistaking the stain of red on her cheek as surely the periphery of her eye witnessed the removal of one boot, then the other…the fall of his trousers…

Naked as a Greek statue, he settled back, arms stretched to either side of him along the back of the settee.

And his cock? Well, it was beginning to make a spectacle of itself as it lay half full against his thigh.

"It doesn't work that way, you know," he said. What was it about this woman that he enjoyed discomfiting her so?

"What doesn't?" Still, she didn't turn.

"You have to look at me to paint me."

She went very still, took a deep breath, and, at last, shifted her body to face him. Her eyes went wide, and she gasped.

Of course, her gaze would go straight *there*.

Chapter Eight

A MELIA HAD SEEN the nude male form.
    In many iterations.

Paintings...statuary...even as a child when she and her siblings would run around naked for entire summers at a time.

She'd known the basics of the male anatomy.

But what greeted her eyes now...

Nothing that came before was anything to *this*.

To Ripon's, um, anatomy.

Muscles everywhere—arms, shoulders, chest, thighs, stomach—rippling beneath skin with a light dusting of dark brown hair. And then there was *that* part... Nothing in her life had properly prepared her for its...*girth*, for lack of a more fitting word.

Neither had anything in her life prepared her for her body's response to the sight of him. While she hadn't the faintest notion of what to do with a man like him, her body seemed to be entertaining ideas, as if she'd been sat to a seven-course supper after thirty days in the desert.

From the pit of her stomach heat expanded within her, as if seeking a way out and finding none. She hadn't the least idea of how to rid herself of it.

But the man inciting this feeling?

He did.

Instinct bade her shift back, to put distance between herself and the naked man who sat not four feet away and appeared utterly unbothered by his nakedness. In fact…was that a glint of challenge in his eyes?

Right.

She noticed the paintbrush in her hand. She was to use it, if only she could remember how.

Again, instinct took over as her brush began to move, starting with the defined line of his clavicle, the subtle indent at the base of his neck, the dusting of hair across his chest, dense muscles beneath, and lower still the eye followed down the packed ridges of his stomach…and lower still…

She left that space blank, for now. She needed distance from *that*—and the curious feeling it lit inside her—to do what they were here for.

Her gaze lifted and followed the long line of an arm, the way shadow and light played against his skin and the bulk of the muscles beneath. In classical statuary, he wouldn't be the David. He would be the Goliath.

A creative passion like she'd never felt ran rampant through her, as if she were infected with a fever that she never wanted to cool.

"Shift your chin down and left just a hair."

A smile that held a hint of wickedness tipped about his mouth as he obeyed. She was commanding him—a duke—and he didn't mind all that much.

"Keep the smile," she said. Some part of her understood there would be a day when she would want to see his smile again. That smile hinted at the essence of the man she was coming to know— the man he truly was. A little bit grouchy. A little bit playful.

Without thinking, she shifted forward and grabbed his wrist to turn it. A second later, it hit her, and she froze in place. She'd breached the distance between them and was *touching* him—this nude man.

She didn't startle. In fact, her hand seemed to refuse to move away from him. As if it would shrivel into nothingness without the feel of him—his skin, muscle, and bone…his heat…his substance… All she wanted was to keep feeling him.

His gaze captured hers. He saw into her, she knew in an instant. These unnamable emotions rioting through her, he knew their names.

And he knew how to satisfy them.

Of its own accord, her hand began tracing up his forearm, banked strength dormant beneath her feathery fingertips. He reached out with his other hand and caressed her cheek, calloused fingertips a light scratch against smooth skin. Oh, she liked the feel of his rough skin against her. She could remain here, inside the spell this man had cast, forever. Except her body ached for *more*—more of his touch, more of *him*. Perhaps *all* of him. Whatever that entailed.

Well, she had an idea. She wasn't a complete dolt.

This man had beguiled her, that was all. No longer was it enough to paint him.

She must *feel* him.

She must *have* him.

"Are you certain?" he asked, his voice the deep velvet rumble that ever sent a shiver purling up her spine.

"Certain of what?" she asked, breathless. She was certain of nothing.

That wasn't true.

She was certain she wanted him.

"Certain of *this*."

He didn't need to explain. Inexperienced she might've been, but she knew what *this* was, and she'd never wanted anything more in all her life.

"I'm not lushy tonight," she said, suddenly awash with nerves. Might he refuse her again? She wouldn't survive it, as it was entirely possible her body would combust into a ball of flame. "You can kiss me."

"Then we shouldn't."

Her entire world dropped out from beneath her. "What do you mean?"

How desperate could she possibly sound? She cared not. She might just beg, if it came to it.

His gaze burned, refusing to release her. "I could never be

satisfied with a single kiss."

"Last night—"

He shook his head slowly. "Last night doesn't count."

He needed her to say something...to prove something. Something that would allow him to relent and give over to this desire pulsing between them. She opted for the truth. "And what makes you think *I* could be satisfied with a single kiss?"

His gaze searched hers, and something unlocked within those silvery gray depths. "It would be ungentlemanly to leave you unsatisfied."

An arrow of pure, carnal, triumphant lust shot through her as his hand reached out and caught the back of her head and drew her forward. She inhaled a tiny sip of air just before his lips met hers. Unlike the rest of him, which was hard and unrelenting, his mouth was soft and tasted of spice and possibly oranges. The man was delicious, and she wanted more.

His tongue skimmed her lips. It was the most erotic sensation of her life and sent a streak of desire straight through her center. Tempted forward, her tongue met his, testingly at first, soft and firm and slick and—*oh*—intoxicating. Then her tongue was in a tangle with his as she fell deep into his kiss, which had the power to turn her into nothing more than a greedy hoyden as she pitched forward on her chair, perched on the very edge for fear of losing contact. Then it was one inch too many and she slipped off the chair and to her knees in an ungraceful tumble.

Yet, somehow, she managed not to break contact as she clutched his shoulders. He smiled against her mouth, and a laugh rumbled deep in his chest, and she wasn't in the least offended. Let him laugh. She rather liked its contrast with the very seriousness of the moment. Because it was a fact. She very seriously desired this man.

He pulled back, his mouth breaking from hers, and a whimpering sound escaped her that would fill her with unbearable shame on the morrow, she hadn't a doubt. But, tonight, she cared not as he stared down at her. He reached out and with a few expert flicks of his fingers, he'd pulled the pins and had her hair tumbling about her shoulders. His hands moved lower and another few flicks had her dress going slack.

With the knowledge of Eve, she met the dark flare of his gaze and knew what to do. His wasn't the only power in this room. She unfolded her too-tall body and stood before him, allowing her dress to fall to the floor. She reached around to untie her stays—she never had them bound tightly—her breasts thrusting forward, her taut nipples showing through her silk chemise. She'd always thought her breasts too small to be attractive. But the look in his eyes indicated the opposite. *Hunger.*

He shifted back against the settee, his gaze raking over her. "Your chemise."

She lifted the garment over her head and let it join dress and stays on the floor, unregarded. She only awaited his next command.

"The stockings can stay."

Stockings or not, Amelia wasn't sure she'd ever been so naked in all her life as his gaze roved across her from head to toe with a slow deliberation. She trembled with awareness and anticipation. No longer could her gaze hold his, not from shyness, but from a corresponding curiosity.

If he was to know every inch of her body, wasn't it only fair that she know every inch of his?

And she knew exactly which inches she wanted to know.

Her gaze drifted down the planes and angles of his body until she found what inches she sought. *Him…*thick and ready…

For her.

He reached for her waist and tugged without force, giving her the option of turning away, of changing her mind. *No.* That wouldn't be the story of this night. Again, he tugged, and this time she swayed forward.

His face angled up, the hand at her waist growing firmer in its hold, more intent, his other hand skimming lightly up her thigh. "You have the longest, most beautiful legs in all creation."

His hand kept moving, over her hip bone, the flat of her stomach, until it cupped one breast. He pulled her forward, and before she knew what he was about his mouth had replaced his hand and his tongue was lazily swirling around her nipple.

Lightning sparks of pleasure streaked through her as she grabbed his shoulders to steady herself before her knees gave out from beneath her. Eyes closed, her head tipped back and a long, slow moan escaped her. She'd never known a mouth on her breasts could create such a commotion of raw need in her body.

The hand clutching her waist moved to her bottom. "Perfection," he murmured against her breast.

A thrill raced through her. She'd long made her peace with the fact that she was more angles than curves, but this man thought some part of her perfection. The idea seduced her as surely as his hands and mouth.

He began trailing kisses up the column of her neck as he drew her closer. Unable to keep the hoyden at bay a second longer, immediacy took over and she inelegantly lurched forward—who had time for elegance?—and climbed atop him so she sat, straddling his thick thighs, her breath coming in short gasps. Later, she would wonder about this daring side that she hadn't known existed until tonight.

But not now.

Now, her gaze met his on an equal plane and the craving she saw in there sent shivers skittering through her. This gorgeous, glorious, too massive, too masculine man wanted her.

And she wanted him.

How simple—how elemental—was desire.

Parched and hungry for him, she took his face in both hands and drew him in for another kiss, her nipples pressing into his chest. She simply needed his mouth on hers. How deep, how complete was her fall into his kiss that she hardly noticed when his hand began trailing up her thighs and slid beneath her. Then she—*oh*—noticed. How her sex throbbed and ached in anticipation of his touch. Rough fingers slid along her slit, and she gasped, more sparks flying through her, her entire being concentrated where he touched her...*there*. Her face angled and her mouth found his neck, the taste of salt and man on her tongue.

"You're so wet, my sweet," came a low murmur in her ear, a long groan pouring from her when he found her center. "And so tight."

She inhaled at the sensation of his long, thick finger entering her. It was a not unpleasant feeling as her sex adjusted around him. With a will of their own, her hips moved in a slow circle and his finger slid in and out of her, in again.

Oh, this feeling...

It was better than prosecco.

"So eager," he rumbled on a laugh.

A novel sense of urgency began to scratch at her. "I need more," she rasped.

"And you shall have it." His gaze went serious. "Touch me."

Oh.

He didn't need to tell her where.

She knew.

Her hand slipped between them, down his muscled chest, ridged stomach—oh, the muscular feel of him—lower until...*oh.* There *he* was. Trembly fingertips feathered down his length.

His head arced back, and a moan escaped him. "Wrap your fingers around me."

She did. The feel of him. *So hard. So big.* She squeezed and tugged. "Like that?"

"Oh, yes, exactly like that."

Sudden, impatient greed clawed at her. She wasn't entirely certain he would fit, but she wanted *this* inside her. *Now.* "Ripon—"

"*Tristan.*"

"Tristan," she repeated. The name of a hero. It suited him. Tonight, she would be his Isolde. "I need *you.*"

His gaze, cloudy with desire, met hers. "You're certain?"

She bit her bottom lip between her teeth and nodded. She'd never been more certain of anything in her life.

His hands tightened on her hips and lifted, her arms draped over his shoulders for balance. His fingers covered hers around his manhood and guided *him* to the entrance of her sex. "This will hurt a bit," he muttered in her ear. "We'll move slow."

She wasn't certain slow was possible. She was simply so hungry for him. With breathless deliberation, she lowered onto him as he stretched her, filling her inch by inch. It did pinch, but alongside the pain raced pleasure.

"Am I too much?" he said against her neck.

Yes. "No."

Somehow her body understood she needed all of him inside her. A need she hadn't been aware of in all of her seven and twenty years. And when she thought she'd surely taken all of him in, there was yet more of him to be had. Her hips moved on him, shallow at first, testingly, the race of her heart in unison with his, their breath mingling inside the curtain of her hair, every movement of her hips eliciting a groan from him. How sweet was the pain of pleasure. A bead of sweat dripped from her chin onto his chest.

"Are you ready?" he asked.

Ready?

"Aren't we...aren't we already...?" She wasn't sure how to finish.

"You have so much to learn, my sweet."

My sweet.

The idea of being *his* was as seductive as the man himself.

His hands tightened on her hips and took control of the movement of her body, the length of him stroking in and out of her in measured rhythm, pain tipping over into pleasure. And the pain that remained? Strangely, it craved more and more as a feeling began to build inside her. A need that was beginning to make demands of her—that she satisfy it. She had no idea how, but the man whose body moved against hers...

He did.

He gathered her closer, only a slick of sweat between them, and she felt permission to give over to abandon as she grabbed his hair and pressed her mouth to his, reduced to the very elements of who she was.

She broke from his mouth. "I never knew it was like this."

His gaze, dark with promise, held hers. "It isn't."

Amelia didn't take his meaning, but she couldn't think in this moment. She could only *be* as he slouched further back onto the settee, thrusting his hips, impaling her further, drawing a gasp from her. "Too much?" he asked.

"I think…"—*oh*—"I think…"—*oh*—"I think it might not be enough."

His mouth curved into a wicked smile. "Insatiable, my sweet."

As one, the rhythm of their hips increased, their bodies moving in perfect counterpoint. Tension coiled tight inside her, pulling at her, demanding focus.

"Amelia," he said, "surrender."

"I…I…I don't know…how." Surrender wasn't in her nature.

"Your body knows."

As she moved on him, the promise of something…something…*more*…scratched at her… Her body tensed… Her quim held… Of a sudden, release burst upon her in a wash of bright orange… Her sex pulsing around his thick manhood, pleasure spiking through her veins in a platinum streak, afloat in the abandon of a wild space that existed outside the realm of that which could be touched.

And still he moved inside her, stroke after relentless stroke.

It was too much.

It would never be enough.

"You are…" he murmured into the base of her throat. The same abandon that had seized her moments ago now held him within its unrelenting grip.

"I am what?" She needed to know.

But he'd lost the thread as he tensed beneath her, the thrust of his manhood, hard and demanding. Amelia could only hold on as he released a long groan and climax took him and he gathered her in his arms, held her tight, and settled back.

Somehow, through sated lips she asked again, "I am what?"

Eyes closed, he grunted.

Her chest pressed to his, she felt the sure beat of his heart, matching her own, each thud slower than the last.

"Unexpected."

"Pardon?" she asked, her cheek now resting against the crook of his neck, eyes closed, her mind and body adrift.

"You are unexpected, Lady Amelia Windermere," she heard, muted, as if from a great distance.

Pleasured and safe in his arms, she fell into complete surrender as never before in her life.

ꙮ

DAWN BLINKING GOLDEN light through parted bed curtains, Amelia stared unblinking at the frescoed ceiling above.

He was gone.

At some hour unknown to her, he'd deposited her into bed and didn't join her.

Though she tugged at his arm.

Though she whimpered.

Of course, with morning returned sanity and a few rational thoughts. Like…

She was no longer a virgin.

Possibly no longer marriageable. Not that she cared about *that* all that much.

While she wanted to be accepted back into proper society, she'd never been all that concerned with ensnaring a husband. Her family already had money and titles, after all.

Even so, she'd also never seen herself as the sort of woman who would take lovers, either.

And she most definitely didn't want to be *seen* as the sort of woman who took lovers.

Just below family, reputation was everything, and the Duke of Ripon would be bad for her reputation. *Very bad.*

Her mind knew this. Her body, however, held a differing position on the subject of the Duke of Ripon, for it had learned something about him only hours ago…

How very, very *good* he was.

She squeezed her thighs together and dragged a pillow across her face.

And groaned.

She may never stop groaning.

So, this was how it felt to have opened Pandora's box?

Chapter Nine

Three days later

THE SUN POURED heat into a countryside unencumbered by a single cloud in the sky. Tristan let it soak into him as he allowed his silver bay to alternate between a trot and a canter according to its own mood. This was the sort of day one left England for.

Only this morning, he'd received an invitation from Lord Archer to join his party for an outing in the Chianti Hills.

It will be a lark, and there will be opera singers.

Tristan had snorted and thought about tossing the invitation into the rubbish. After all, he was a known recluse, his refusal would only be expected. Further, he wasn't particularly keen on joining a Windermere party—with opera singers—in the countryside. Not in the plural sense, anyway.

But in the singular—as in one particular Windermere…

He was very much interested.

It had been three days, and he couldn't get the blasted woman out of his mind. He'd tried sculpting her from memory—the elegant column of her neck…the delicate line of her clavicle…the exquisite turn of her wrist…and other parts, too. Parts only a lover would know. The feminine indent of her waist. The subtle flare of her hips. The firm curve of her derriere. The sweet perfection of her breasts. His tongue could still taste the salt of her.

He'd thought he could sculpt the memory of her into submission. But it refused to submit, instead insisting on dominating his every waking hour, and his sleeping ones, too.

He'd had no choice but to accept her brother's invitation. He must see her again, if only to rid himself of the memory of her. Or...

Was it to form new memories of her?

Was he truly so weak?

It was entirely possible.

For here was the thing: he'd taken her virginity. *That* had been weakness, of the mind and body, no matter that she'd had a choice in the matter. He should've known better. He *did* know better.

So, why was he actually here?

To right a situation that had gotten out of hand?

Bloody hell.

The bay topped the hill they'd been climbing this last quarter hour, and Tristan tugged the reins to take in the view. The Chianti Hills rolled soft and green and brown all around him, some hills wild with tall grasses and woodland, others tamed by the grape vines that the hills gave their name. Though the area lacked the hustle and bustle of the city, no few people passed him on his ride. The odd donkey cart. Pairs of women on foot, walking to the nearest village or visiting a neighbor.

This was the pace of life for Tristan. When he returned to England in just a few months, he'd decided he would be spending the majority of the year at the family seat in Gloucestershire. He rather thought he would enjoy it, too. Italy had taught him something about the pleasures in life. It wasn't one's physical location that mattered as much as what one carried inside them.

Or was it someone who had taught him that?

"Ripon!" came a shout.

Not a hundred yards distant, in the middle of a field, lounged Lord Archer, waving, his curls shining platinum beneath the unrelenting sun. This must be the Windermere picnic spot. He could see why with the view of rolling hills and even the white glint of the Florentine duomo in the distance. Tristan dismounted from his bay and handed over the reins to a servant before walking over to Archer and his friend Lord Kilmuir. Tristan knew the latter as a nodding acquaintance from Eton many years ago, not much more than that. But even he could see the man had taken a turn for the morose, which Archer seemed utterly unbothered by.

Woman troubles, no doubt.

Tristan glanced around and found no sign of anyone else. Had he misunderstood Archer's invitation?

"Any trouble finding us?" asked Archer, already extending a cup of something surely intoxicating toward Tristan.

"None at all."

He continued to cast his gaze about. Toward the nearest grove of olive trees. Across the plain of tall grass stretching down the hill. Not a trace of another Windermere.

Not a trace of *her*.

Disappointment stole through him. What was he doing here? He hadn't the faintest interest in drinking the afternoon away with Archer and his morose friend. He saw but one way forward—the direct. "Is it only the three of us in the party?"

"Oh, no, the women have struck off in a ramble. Scattered amongst the hills like dandelions." Archer didn't seem too concerned. "And thank God for that."

"Oh?" asked Tristan.

Archer popped a grape into his mouth and spoke around it, "Amelia received a letter from England this morning that's got her all in a tizzy."

Kilmuir pushed to a stand. "I'm off on a ramble meself," he said in his light Scottish burr.

"But Ravensworth will be here any minute with opera singers," said Archer.

Kilmuir grunted and stalked off toward the olive trees.

Just then came the sound of carriage wheels crunching across dirt and gravel, accompanied by a wafting of feminine laughter. Tristan caught a glimpse of ostrich feathers. Ravensworth and the opera singers had arrived.

Tristan took that as his cue to embark on a ramble himself and told Archer as much.

"But the opera singers, Ripon," said Archer.

"More for you," said Tristan and tipped his hat. He headed in the direction opposite the one taken by Kilmuir. No morose Scotsmen for him today.

Across the tall grass he strode. This was no lazy afternoon ramble. He had a woman to find.

On the other side of a thin blade of cherry laurels and halfway down a small hillside, he caught sight of two female figures on a blanket—one with silky raven-black hair and the other with a riot of short blonde curls. His heart performed a neat little flip in his chest before his mind caught up with the reaction. Lady Amelia had long, flowing curls. This was Lady Delilah and their cousin Miss Windermere.

"If it isn't the Duke of Ripon," called out Lady Delilah, holding a hand to her forehead. "How interesting to see you here." Both women stared at him with matching curious expressions.

"Just here for an afternoon ramble."

Their heads canted at the exact same angle. They weren't convinced. "Tell me, Your Grace," continued Lady Delilah, "what is your opinion of Christopher Marlowe?"

"The playwright?" A conversation with the Windermeres certainly never took the usual turn.

As one, the ladies nodded.

He had a feeling there was a correct answer, and he wasn't about to deliver it. "I haven't one."

He gave them a tip of the hat and was on his way.

"If you see Amelia, give her our regards."

A flurry of soft giggles might have met his back. No matter. Lady Amelia was near. He sensed it.

Just inside an oak woodland at the bottom of yet another hill, he encountered a narrow stream. Instinct had him cutting left and following its shallow bank upstream. If he knew Lady Amelia Windermere at all—and he did, quite well—she would be situated alongside the mellow trickle of water flowing lazily over rocks and moss with a charcoal or paintbrush in her hand.

He rounded a bend and found her not thirty feet away just as he'd imagined her: tucked in a little patch of grass beside the water, green checked blanket spread beneath her, charcoal in hand, sketchbook on her lap, gaze both dreamy and focused, lost in the state of creation. She must have caught movement in the corner of her eye for her gaze flicked up and held his. He kept placing one foot in front of the other until he reached the edge of her blanket.

She looked a vision, Lady Amelia Windermere, in her mint-green sprigged muslin dress and hair tied loosely back, her curls having their own ideas about their bound state. In truth, she looked like a woman waiting to be ravished. Which, of course, she wasn't. But the way she was staring up at him...

Or was she?

With care, she set her sketching materials off to the side and pushed to a stand. No words had yet been spoken, but they didn't seem all that necessary. Between them lay not five feet which she crossed with a few steps; now separated by mere inches, a light blush staining her cheeks, her mouth parted in an upturned O, her delicate, crisp scent of lavender just reaching him. Her breath came in shallow bursts as if she'd run a great distance.

She reached a tentative hand out and caressed his cheek while pressing the flat of her other palm against his chest, his heart a gallop against his ribs. How he'd craved her touch these last three days. Ached for it, in fact. But his body was greedy and wanted more than the caress of a cheek.

It wanted all of her.

But it was hers to give, not his to take.

She lifted to the tips of her toes and touched soft lips to his, her hands finding the back of his head, her fingernails a light scrape across his scalp. Goose bumps lifted across his skin as he found the small of her back and pressed her up against the length of his body, deepening the kiss. Still, no words had passed their lips, but their bodies knew what to say.

All at once, tentativeness transformed into greed. She was pushing his coat off his shoulders and unknotting his cravat. He was blindly searching for the buttons of her bodice and sorely tempted to rip them off when they refused to give way. She'd become frustrated with the buttons of his waistcoat and had no such qualms, one button flying into the grass, another plunking into the stream.

He couldn't remember ever feeling this frantic need for a woman, to have her touch upon him, to have her flesh made one with his. Through the gray superfine of his trousers, her fingers traced the hard length of his manhood. He sucked in a sharp breath. *Help him.*

As she fumbled about the closure, he had her stays unbound and the chemise over her head before removing his own shirt. Her gaze fixed on the view before her, and her fingers went still. "I never knew men of flesh and blood looked like you."

And he understood at once something he'd liked about her from the very beginning.

This woman didn't see him as a duke.

But as a *man.*

It mattered.

The suspicion entered that he might more than like this woman.

Even if she didn't know how to operate the closure of a man's trousers. They would be here all day—completely, frantically unsatisfied—if he left it up to her. So, he did the only sensible thing and brushed her fingers aside before finishing the job himself. Then he gathered her in his arms and laid them both down onto the blanket.

Stretched beneath him, golden curls tumbled about her, she was a vision. Only her stockings and slippers remained. Today, they must go. He would never forgive himself if he went another day without seeing those perfect legs unclad.

Stockings flung away, possibly into a tree, he skimmed up the long length of her legs with fingertips and tongue, savoring the taste of her, the sun illuminating pale skin through the dappled canopy above. Her fingers wove through his hair, tugging at him until they met eye to eye, him above and she below.

"I can't wait a second longer," she whispered. "I ache for you."

Her arms wrapped around his neck, and her legs around his waist, snugging her body against his, her taut nipples poking against his chest, her sex slick against his cock. Her eyes drifted shut, and she moaned, liquid and languorous, as she moved against his hard length. Her movement a tease…a *promise*.

He couldn't take anymore. He took his length in hand and guided himself to the entrance of her sweet, wet quim.

I ache for you.

He knew he must take his time. With one long, possessive stroke he took her, watching her face wince with a tiny shard of pain, then blossom with pleasure, as he filled her, inch by deliberate inch. She gasped. She groaned. He remained steady, even when she began moving against him with unpracticed movements that drove him wild for her.

Sensing that she'd adjusted to him, he found a rhythm with her. Her inhalations deepened and her groans lengthened and her grip tightened on his arse, her legs splaying wider, demanding *more*. Her honest craving for him lacked artifice or pretense. The sincerity of it snuck past his defenses and touched a place inside him he didn't want to exist. He and Amelia, together, wasn't a flat, soulless coupling. It held depth and dimension. It might be something worth holding onto.

His weight supported by a forearm to the side of her head, his other hand reached beneath her bottom and lifted so her hips now angled up.

"There's more of you?" she asked on a gasp, even as a wicked smile tipped about her mouth.

He chuckled, continuing to deliver stroke after intentioned stroke.

"Oh, Tristan," she cried out, and gratification soared through him.

His mouth found the crook of her neck and licked. A long, animal moan escaped her. His tongue trailed lower, hungry for the taste of her—*lavender…salt…woman.*

He reached beneath her shoulders and brought her so her breasts met his mouth. The woman had the most perfect, little breasts. He couldn't get enough as he kissed, licked, and sucked them, encouraging her to become her wildest self beneath him. She'd gone mindless with abandon.

His, the primal beast within him demanded…*claimed.*

Her eyes squeezed shut, and she bit her bottom lip between her teeth, her movements becoming more focused. She was seeking release.

He could give it to her like this, but there was another way he wanted to experience her.

Using what little willpower that yet existed inside him, he pulled from her. Her eyes flew open. "What are you doing?" she demanded.

As he moved down her body, he smiled up at her. "You'll see."

She looked not one bit convinced.

She would be.

Her mouth parted with both alarm and curiosity. "Tristan, are you about to—"

He stroked up the length of her slit with his tongue and stole the question from her mouth. Two fingers entered her, and his tongue found the nub of her sex. He took himself in hand and stroked his hard length as he worked her body. She was already growing wild beneath him as her long, perfect legs wrapped around his head. This wouldn't take long.

She inhaled a sharp gasp and tensed beneath him, but his tongue and fingers didn't let up. Then she broke, her sex quivering delicately beneath and around him. A few more strokes of his manhood and climax washed over him, sending him over the edge as an animal roar poured forth.

Heart pounding, pleasure coursing through his veins with each sated thud, he rolled off her, taking one of her legs with him, holding it close as he collapsed onto his back. Together, they lay, blanket at their backs, staring up at the blue sky peeking through the tree canopy. A light breeze cooling the sweat off their skin, this was bliss, pure and simple.

Through the sound of leaves rustling, birds trilling, and stream flowing came her voice. "I once thought a man's buttocks couldn't possibly be as muscular and taut as that of the statue of David."

"And now?"

"I was wrong."

He chuckled, the sound a deep, warm rumble that invited her in.

Her serious gaze met his. "I'm not sure of who I am with you. It's not who I thought I was."

That made two of them.

He wasn't sure if it was a comfort.

AMELIA RECLAIMED HER leg from Tristan and sat up. She needed to think, and that ability was severely hampered when this man was touching her.

They'd done *it…again*.

Once could be called a mistake.

But twice?

Twice had the beginnings of a pattern.

He rolled onto his side. His eyes held an unknown quality. It made her nervous.

"We should dress." She reached for her chemise to prove her point.

"Why?" he asked.

That *why* was the spark of irritation she needed. But, really, sometimes the man could be such a *duke*. "Before we're discovered," she said, as if it needed saying.

He rolled onto his back, one arm draped across his face, utterly, unabashedly unbothered.

Oh, the naked sight of him.

She couldn't look at the naked sight of him.

Not if she was to keep her hands off him.

"You could stay," he muttered, one eye peeking up at her.

"Stay?"

"Stay."

"In Italy?"

That wasn't part of her plan.

At all.

"With me."

Oh.

"Stay...in Italy...with *you*." The words refused to sink into her brain. "As what? Your mistress?"

He sat up and reached for his trousers. Her hoyden side wished he wouldn't, but her sensible side sensed the coming conversation called for a few articles of clothing. She slipped the chemise over her head. Clad in his trousers, he faced her. She tried to keep her gaze on his, but his bare chest was calling out to be gazed upon and adored.

"You could be my mistress if you like," he said.

Outrage should be tearing through her, but...it wasn't.

"You could cultivate a bohemian reputation," he continued. "You're nearly there if half the gossip about your family is true."

"You listen to gossip?"

He snorted. "Listen might be a stretch."

Of a sudden, she understood something. "I don't want to be your mistress."

Her refusal changed nothing between them. If anything, the look in his eyes told her he'd expected as much.

"Would you prefer to be my wife?"

Before the import of the question could sink in, he continued, "You were a virgin, and I've come to my senses."

"I rather think it was our senses that got us carried away."

His gaze remained serious. "No word play," he growled.

She supposed he was right. How quickly a frolic in the woods could turn into serious business. She reached for her stays, and he for his shirt.

A *wife*. The wife of a *duke*...

Wasn't that what she wanted? Wouldn't it assure her place in society?

But like this? It seemed so...

Shabby.

She shook her head. "Not your wife."

He ran an exasperated hand through his hair. "Then what do you want, woman?"

She inhaled and reached for her sketchbook. A slip of paper slid from the back pages. "I've had a plan, and it's finally worked," she said and handed the paper over to him.

He gave the contents a quick scan. Contents she'd already memorized. At last, all of her efforts to reclaim her and her siblings' place in society had borne fruit. They were now in possession of the most exclusive invitation of the London Season: the Marchioness of Sutton's season-end ball.

Tristan let the paper fall onto the stretch of blanket between them. He looked wholly flummoxed. "You're returning to England to attend a ball?"

"It's more than a ball." She slightly resented having to explain this to a man who would never understand. "I've been working on securing this invitation for nearly a year." She didn't sound happy about it. In fact, she might sound wretched.

He snorted.

It was all she needed. "You truly have no appreciation for a woman's place in the world, do you?" She reached for her stockings and decided against them, instead stuffing them into her valise.

"How do you mean?"

"With the Windermere reputation in shreds, how do you expect Delilah and Juliet to secure marriage proposals from gentlemen of good families?"

He was regarding her with absolute incredulity. "And what about you?" he demanded. "You've just received a proposal of marriage from a gentleman of good family—a duke, moreover— and you've refused it."

"That is different."

"How so?"

"It simply is."

Tristan shot to his feet, clearly exasperated. He pointed at her. "You care too much what people think."

Now it was her shooting to her feet. "And you care too little."

They stood facing each other, half-undressed, like adversaries.

"Not all of us can live in infamy ever after, Your Grace," she spat.

"But, Amelia," he said, his tone softening and possibly thawing something inside her, "it's the only way to live happily. What do you need the opinion of a few dried-up crones for? You're an artist."

Her gaze skittered away and settled unseeing on the stream. "I'm a lady who dabbles in watercolor."

"You're an artist," he repeated, "and somewhere beneath the empty words you're spouting at me, you know it. I've seen her." A beat. "I've seen *you*. Don't give up on yourself just yet. Tear up the invitation. Live in infamy with me."

And she saw they weren't adversaries; they never had been.

They were twice lovers, and that was all they ever could be, for he was asking of her something she couldn't give.

She must reenter society. For herself. For her family. She couldn't miss the opportunity.

Yet, still, he persisted. He might even be begging. "You don't seem to understand something about yourself that I do. You're a passionate woman, Amelia. Tell me, when has society ever had any use for a passionate woman? Just ask Lady Caroline Lamb how she's faring."

He jerked on the remainder of his clothes. Amelia did the same at a slower pace, half a watchful eye on him.

Just before he stalked away, he asked, "When do you leave?"

"In two days." That would give them enough time to pack their belongings and make it back to England a fortnight or so before Lady Sutton's ball.

His jaw clenched, and he nodded before pivoting on his heel.

Amelia had no choice but to watch until he disappeared from view. She grabbed the invitation and read it for the dozenth time. She should feel a happy sense of accomplishment. She'd worked every single one of her friends, relatives, and even acquaintances to assist her in the procurement of this very thing. Yet, instead, she felt very close to wretched.

She gathered her things and began making her way back to Delilah and Juliet, but soon found they weren't where she'd left them. So, she kept walking and trying to rid her mind of the last half hour of her life.

Easier said than done.

Ahead, a flurry of movement caught her eye. Juliet emerged from a small grove of olive trees looking quite unlike herself.

Gone was her usual observant placidity. In its place was a face like thunder.

"Juliet!" she called out, alarmed.

Juliet's head whipped around. Her eyes were suspiciously shiny. Were those tears? Amelia had never seen Juliet cry, not even as a small child.

"Is something the matter?" she asked, closing the distance between them and taking her cousin's hand.

Before Juliet could reply, another figure emerged from the woods. *Kilmuir.* He looked slightly confused and no small bit bewildered.

The alarm inside Amelia grew in volume. "Juliet," she began, gingerly, "did he do something to you?"

A laugh that sounded suspiciously bitter emerged from Juliet. "He did nothing. As always, Kilmuir is the picture of gentleman-liness."

Amelia chose her next words carefully. "It's that you look terribly upset."

A bright smile spread across Juliet's face that didn't quite reach her eyes. "I am perfectly, perfectly well. Never better, in fact."

Her gaze swept over Amelia as if only now seeing her. Her eyebrows crinkled together. Amelia must look an absolute frumpled mess. She'd never been all that adept at dressing herself. "And you, cousin, are you well?"

Amelia returned the smile Juliet had given her. The one that wouldn't quite reach her eyes. "Perfectly so."

And on they walked in silence, each in their own thoughts.

Amelia felt she was, in fact, doing perfectly well for a woman who'd tupped a duke twice, then refused his proposal of marriage. A duke who made her body come alive in inconceivable ways.

The weight of Lady Sutton's invitation sat heavy in her bag.

Amelia couldn't lose sight of what was important. She'd attained her goal at last in securing that invitation. She'd ensured that she, Archie, Delilah, and Juliet would be received into the best society before Mama and Papa returned from Samarkand.

She couldn't miss this opportunity. To do so would be letting her family down, even if they didn't seem to appreciate it.

Also, she would be letting herself down if she didn't follow through. She'd worked most scrupulously for this. Lady Sutton's ball would be her victory lap.

She must do what was right.

Even if her body screamed in protest all the way back to England.

Chapter Ten

London
Six weeks later

TRISTAN'S FATHER AND his father's father and his father's father's father had all surely set arse on the wide leather armchair presently hosting his own arse, newspaper spread before him, crystal tumbler in hand, two fingers of brandy inside, attentive staff on high alert to refill at the subtlest lift of his eyebrow. Such was the privilege of a duke in a gentleman's club such as Brooks's, whose sole purpose was to cater to his every need and whim.

He'd been back in London for less than a week and was already chafing at Town life. But he had no one else to blame. He'd chosen to return four months earlier than was strictly, absolutely necessary.

And why had he done it? He'd been asking himself that question from the very moment he'd made the decision to journey home. He always arrived at the same answer.

Because of *her*.

It was a fact.

He'd followed Lady Amelia Windermere from Italy.

Another fact that kept taunting him?

The reason *why*.

He was very likely smitten with the woman.

He'd vowed never to put himself in such a position, but here he was, feeling slightly wretched, unable to eat more than a few bites of any meal, and decidedly grouchy about it all. He couldn't understand what it was about this state of being that invoked rhapsodies of verse from poets. Lovesickness was a decidedly pitiable state.

Which, of course, didn't mean he had any intention of acting upon it. She'd very firmly refused his proposal of marriage. Yet…

He'd followed her.

It was a paradox.

"Ripon!" he heard for at least the thirtieth time in as many minutes. Yet another old school chum. London abounded with them. It was quickly returning to Tristan what it was to lead the life of a man-about-town. *Blasted boring.*

"Ripon," came his name yet again. This time, it was a voice he'd heard more recently than ten years ago.

He lifted his gaze to find the Duke of Ravensworth weaving his way across Persian carpets. Blonde hair muted beneath the low light of dim lamps and customary sardonic twist to his mouth, Ravensworth commanded nods of respect and deference as he neared Tristan. Not many spoke to the Duke of Ravensworth until they were spoken to.

"Ravensworth," said Tristan. He liked the man. He took his responsibilities seriously, and perhaps himself a touch much, but what else did one expect from a duke? After all, they were treated as demigods from their moment of birth. It was a rare occurrence, in fact, to meet a duke who wasn't entirely insufferable.

He snorted. He knew of one person who would place him in the category of Insufferable Duke: the woman with whom he was smitten. What was she doing this very moment? Though he wasn't familiar with the Windermere address—he hadn't allowed himself to inquire, or he might find himself driving past at odd hours of the day and night—he would wager she was no more than two miles from where he currently sat.

And he knew what she was doing.

Readying herself for her triumphant return to society—at the Marchioness of Sutton's ball.

He consulted his pocket watch. The most eager guests would've already started arriving.

Ravensworth took the armchair opposite and signaled for a

brandy. "How do you find our fair homeland of Albion after such a prolonged absence?"

Tristan snorted. "Entirely unchanged."

Ravensworth accepted his drink from the waiter and held it up in a toast. "To our stubborn England."

Tristan took a swig. "Last I saw you was in the Italian countryside, occupying a barouche full of opera singers."

A faraway look entered Ravensworth's eye. "Ah, Italy. How I miss her." His gaze narrowed on Tristan. "And you? After five years, England must come as a bit of a soggy shock."

"It is, and it isn't," said Tristan. "I left needing a different kind of life."

Ravensworth nodded, discerning in his eyes. Tristan realized that if anyone could understand, it would be this man—a man who had been a duke from the moment of his birth.

"But now that I've returned," Tristan continued. "I think maybe I've brought what I need from that life back with me." A beat. "But also I feel ready for a life different from those other two lives."

"The next chapter."

Tristan nodded. That was it exactly. Though he wasn't certain what that chapter entailed precisely, a certain face kept appearing in his mind when he thought about it.

He shook the image away.

She'd said no.

"Our mutual friends the Windermeres are in Town," said Ravensworth, as if he'd peered into Tristan's mind.

"Oh?" Tristan tried to sound aloof.

"They arrived about a fortnight ago."

"Hmm." This wasn't new information.

"Interesting timing that you returned only a few days later."

Tristan didn't like the way Ravensworth was watching him, as if he knew something.

"Is it?" Tristan wouldn't be sharing the details—or secrets—of his interior life with Ravensworth.

"They're attending the Marchioness of Sutton's ball tonight."

"There is no shortage of nightly entertainments this time of year," said Tristan coolly.

"I'm giving it a pass," said Ravensworth. "You?"

"I hadn't given it much thought."

He couldn't very well say it was, in fact, all he'd been able to think about from the moment his eyes had opened this morning.

"Lady Amelia worked diligently for this night," continued Ravensworth. "It's almost a shame to miss her triumphant return."

Tristan grunted, but the gears of his mind turned over a few times before a realization walloped him over the head.

He wanted to witness the moment of Amelia's triumph.

He wanted to see her get what she wanted, even if it wasn't him. Then perhaps he'd be able to move on from this inconvenient adoration he'd developed for her.

And he had the perfect excuse. Mother would be attending the Marchioness of Sutton's ball as the two women had been bosom friends since their come-out. While he had no interest in putting himself in the line of sight of matchmaking mamas, his mother would likely appreciate the escort of her only son.

He shot to his feet. "Ravensworth, good seeing you made it back to England all in one piece, but I realize I'm late for an appointment."

A knowing glint in his eye, Ravensworth gave a nod. The man might understand too much.

NOT TWO HOURS later, Tristan found himself entering the Marchioness of Sutton's glittering season-end ball with his mother on his arm. As the ballroom opened before them, he began scanning the room for Amelia. She would be the brightest diamond in a room full of rhinestones.

Mother pulled his arm close. "Can you imagine my shock, Tristan," she began, accepting a coupe of punch from a servant, "when you arrived at my front door to play the gallant escort tonight? To a ball, no less?"

He grunted. She was teasing, and he deserved it. "The marchioness is waving for your attention," he said. He'd thought she would go her own way once they arrived.

"She can wait," said Mother. "Take a turn about the ballroom with me first."

Tristan had known that tone all his life. A capital 'C' conversation was coming. When he'd arrived home a week ago, they'd caught up on five years' worth of business and dined together every evening since. So, it wasn't as if they hadn't spoken in all that time or lacked opportunity. But it was a different sort of conversation Mother was determined to have tonight, and in truth, it was the conversation he'd long needed to have with her, though he hadn't known it until this very moment.

"I suppose you'll tell me what this is all about?" she asked conversationally while they walked. Hers was the smile of a woman secure in her place in the world as she nodded at friends and acquaintances.

"A nice evening with my mother?" he asked, purposely evasive.

"Try again."

A strange moment for him to ask of his mother the question he'd needed to ask her his entire adult life, but here they were. "I need to ask you something." A beat. "About you and Father."

"Ask anything." She was ready.

"You never recovered."

"That's not a question." She smiled, even though melancholy shone from her eyes. "But I understand what you're not asking. The love your father and I shared was deep and true, but I did recover."

He tried not to let his surprise show. "You never remarried."

She met his gaze. "There are other ways to recover from the sort of loss that tries to devastate. I took to running the estates during your minority, and even these last five years." She hesitated. "And while I might not have remarried or found another great love like the one I shared with your father, I did have lovers."

Tristan only just didn't groan. "I'm not sure I need to hear this."

"I think you might," she said. "I've had discreet companion-ship over the years. I'm neither a nun nor a saint. I'm merely human, and I'm not a martyr to my love for William." She gave his arm a squeeze. "Though you were but a babe, your father's untimely death affected the trajectory of both our lives, but I fear you've taken the wrong lesson from my adoration of William. It was the blessing of my life to have had him for five years. His memory is a blessing to me every single day." She swiped away an errant tear. "But it is time, my son, that you open yourself to the blessing only true love can deliver. I thought perhaps—hoped, even—it would happen in Italy."

Tristan grunted. The image of a face appeared in his mind—*her* face.

His mother gave him a quick buss on the cheek. "Think upon what I've said. Your happiness depends upon it." With that, she left him, weaving her way through the crowded ballroom toward her friend, the Marchioness of Sutton.

Strangely, he felt as if a physical weight had been lifted off his shoulders, one he'd been carrying his entire life. Mother was content and fulfilled, and further she'd led a full life. Not the half life he'd always thought, but one where, unafraid, she'd sought and found her own happiness.

Now it was his turn to follow her lead. Though it did occur to him that he'd likely bungled his chance in Italy.

Again, he scanned the ballroom, his height allowing him an unimpeded view. No sign of unruly platinum curls anywhere.

"Ripon!" came a voice with the sound of Eton about it. Yet another old school chum. They seemed to be multiplying, for he found himself surrounded by five or so of them. "Join us in the card room. Old Flicksy is getting a game of loo going."

Tristan opened his mouth to refuse and closed it. If he didn't go with these men to the card room, then his only other option was to stand here like a lovesick swain and become an object of attack for the matchmaking mamas who had begun to cast calculating glances in his direction. Better to retreat now.

And, really, when he thought about it, what had he expected to say to Amelia as she basked in her moment of triumph?

Propose marriage again?

He snorted. Not bloody likely.

She'd made her feelings on that matter very clear.

Impossibly, he grew grouchier. He would turn into a bear by the end of the night at this rate.

So, he nodded and took himself off to the card room, even if he might've given the ballroom one last quick scan on his way out.

Chapter Eleven

A MELIA STEPPED INSIDE the Marchioness of Sutton's sparkling ballroom that positively bounced to the rhythm of stringed instruments and waited for it.

For a sense of accomplishment to sweep over her.

After all, she'd done it. Her letters, letters, and more letters over the last year had paid off, and her family had, at last, gained an entrée back into the glittering heart of society before Mama and Papa returned from Samarkand.

The last year in Italy need never be mentioned again.

Of course, it wasn't what could be mentioned about Italy that occupied her thoughts at least three times a day and haunted her dreams at night. Even her paintbrush wasn't immune as it insisted its only muse was *him*. Frustrating paintbrush.

No matter. This was her moment, and she should bask in it. Instead, she felt a bit deflated. She'd made the Herculean effort to reclaim the Windermeres' right place in society for herself, yes, but for her family, too, and they didn't appreciate it one single bit. Delilah and Juliet had declined to come to the ball altogether, and Archie only agreed when her imploring had turned into begging, and even then he'd deserted her for the card room the instant after their names had been announced. Truly, her family were a bunch of ingrates.

Still, a quiet, sobering thought came to her. Perhaps it was simply that the life she wanted for her family wasn't the one they wanted for themselves. And—here was the truly sobering part—wasn't that their prerogative?

Another sobering thought followed on that one's heels. She'd been so fixed on securing this night that she'd turned down the other life she'd been offered. The one with the Duke of Ripon.

Inexplicable tears sprang to her eyes. They'd made a habit of doing that lately. She couldn't think about *him*, not now, not in the midst of the ball of the season as she stood at its periphery, alone, a carefully trained vacuous smile on her face. She wasn't exactly feeling the warm embrace of society at her return. In fact, it appeared to have gotten along just fine without her. Or had it always been like this, prickly and cold?

A bead of perspiration trickled down her spine, and she saw the ball and its gaiety—some false and some true—in a way she'd never seen a ball: as a hot, stuffy affair with too many not-thoroughly-washed bodies crammed too close together. Certainly, the chandeliers sparkled and the laughter rang bright, but it felt *empty*.

And she couldn't help thinking it might have something to do with that other life she'd been offered.

The one she'd refused.

The one with *him*.

She made for the punch table. She needed something to do and sipping a cup of punch with this vacuous smile on her face would suffice until something better came along.

Snippets of conversation from groupings of ladies floated around her, but none invited her to partake. She had the strange sensation of invisibility. Then came a word that shot through her as solidly as a blunt object.

Ripon.

Her smile slipped, and her ears strained for more.

"The Dissolute Duke, here?" asked the one female voice.

"That's what I heard," said the other.

In a sudden panic, Amelia's gaze searched from one end of the ballroom to the other. Surely, she would know if he was here, sharing the same air as her. But she found no sign of him. So, she did the only sensible thing and sidled closer to the two gossiping ladies.

"Still unmarried?"

"*And* still eminently eligible."

"I never did believe the rumors about him."

"Oh, pish," dismissed the one lady, "even if it was true, who would give a fig? Lady Sarah Locksley had to have been looking for a reason to beg off if that scared her away so easily. One plants one's feet and fights for a man like that."

Amelia considered the lady might have a point.

"I wonder if he's still…"

"The most devastating man on two feet?"

"Those shoulders."

"Those *thighs*."

A warm shiver slid through Amelia. She knew all about those thighs. But the way the ladies stood assessing Tristan rubbed her fur the wrong direction. They spoke of him like he was an object—a desirable object—but an object all the same. A duke…a *thing*…to be caught and possessed.

Of a sudden, she understood the allure of his life in Italy. There, he could be nothing more or less than a man.

He'd been correct about the people populating this ballroom. *Small-minded…judgmental…incurious.*

All of them added together weren't worth one of him.

Oh, what had she done?

Then she heard it. Another name. *Hers.*

She swiveled around to find a grouping of four young ladies staring at her in a manner that neither warmed nor welcomed her. Two of them looked vaguely familiar, but she didn't know any of them by name, much less well enough to have caused the offense that would warrant the looks she was receiving. She tried smiling. They simply kept staring. Then they clustered together to form a tight, little circle.

Amelia's cheeks went hot. She understood precisely what had just happened. She'd received the cut direct. The past misdeeds of her family had neither been forgiven nor forgotten. She felt as exposed as if she stood stark naked with a hundred pairs of eyes upon her.

She glanced around. They weren't. But really, she no longer wanted to be here.

This had been a mistake.

A throat cleared behind her. A masculine throat that sounded too familiar. But surely that was her imagination carrying her away. She turned. Before her stood—

She blinked, unable to believe her eyes.

Before her stood *him*—the ox...the Duke of Ripon...*Tristan*—dressed in evening blacks, his massive, muscular form, improbably congruous with the elegance of his clothing. He looked every inch the devastating duke.

The most devastating man on two feet.

"What are you doing here?" she blurted before thinking better of it. In truth, they'd never been properly introduced, so she shouldn't be speaking any words to him. Further, her words shouldn't have been those words.

"I was hoping you would do me the honor of this dance," he said, formally, correctly.

No few curious glances flicked their direction, and the young ladies who had aimed the cut direct at her might be staring with mouths slightly agape. It shouldn't, but it gave Amelia no small bit of satisfaction. Even so...

She and Tristan most definitely should *not* dance.

She'd vowed never to touch the man again.

She had trouble stopping once she started.

He took a step closer, the space between them not quite intimate, but personal. Only for them. "What just happened with those young ladies?"

"I don't know what you're referring to." Her cheeks flamed with the lie.

"It will keep happening unless..."

He didn't need to finish the sentence. She finished it for him. "I dance with you?" she scoffed with more bravado than she'd thought herself capable. "Why? Because you're my savior?"

What arrogance. The very idea.

"No," he said, coolly. "Because I'm a duke."

It was the irrefutable truth, and they both knew it. A dance with the Duke of Ripon might set a few tongues wagging, but it gave her firmer social standing to be seen as in the favor of such a powerful man.

She dipped in a shallow curtsy as she said, "I would be delighted, Your Grace," and took his hand, allowing herself to be led onto the mahogany dancing floor. The instant he set their bodies in motion to the rhythm of the waltz, she knew: what had happened in Italy hadn't stayed in Italy.

It had followed them here, to London, to this dancing floor, and sizzled between them, made it impossible for her to draw a proper breath.

Or a proper thought.

Oh, Italy, what had it done to her?

He stared down at her, and she knew she must say something with his mouth only inches from hers. She'd never been this close to it without kissing those firm lips. She cleared her throat. "I never took you for the sort of gentleman who fills out young ladies' dance cards."

"I'm not." He snorted. "Older ladies on the other hand..."

Indignation surged up. "Are you implying that I'm no longer a young—"

His mouth tipped into a lopsided smile, and she snapped her mouth shut.

Oh, the cheek of the man.

She turned her head decidedly away. What a very bad idea this had been.

"I saw your brother in the card room," he said, "and I thought you—" He bit off the rest of the sentence.

Again, a blade of heat struck through her. He'd thought she might be receiving the exact treatment she'd been receiving. And he'd come here for...

Her. This frustrating, devastating man who was whirling her across the dancing floor with expert ease, whose silver gray gaze sparked places alight inside her that were better not sparked alight in public, melted something within her. In his arms, in front of all the *ton*, she was safe. The security she'd been attempting to achieve for herself and her family this last year, it was here, in his arms.

Arms that she wanted to gather her closer. She saw the same desire reflected back in his eyes. Of a sudden, she wished they were still in Italy where her hand could remain in his after the waltz ended and they could find a quiet place to—

Talk?

Not even remotely close.

They neared the double doors thrown open to allow cool night air inside the ballroom. Impulse found its voice, and she spoke low enough for his ears only. "Dance me into the garden."

His gaze held hers for the space of a few rapid heartbeats. "No fountains."

A laugh hiccupped out of her, again drawing no few glances. The Lady Amelia Windermere who had left for Italy had never drawn an askance glance in all her life, but the one who had returned... She was rather making a habit of it.

And she wasn't sure she minded.

Live in infamy with me.

Of a sudden, those words held an appeal, hypnotic and *right*, as he whirled her onto the terrace. He held her hand and led her down a short flight of steps and around the side of the mansion. No one could see them here. Music and ballroom chatter faded, leaving only the sound of their breath.

She reached her arms around his neck, and he closed all distance between them, pressing her against the wall, the length of his body against her, and his mouth, at last, claimed hers and all went right with the world.

How desperate she'd been all these weeks for his kiss, for his large, strong hands upon her. She wanted all of him at once, but he smiled against her mouth and slowed her urgency. She released an impatient groan as every movement of his lips and tongue became deliberate and intentional.

Restless desire poured through her as her hands roved down his muscled chest, his ridged stomach, until they reached *him*, the length of his manhood, hard and ready, straining against his trousers. Insatiable fingertips grazed across superfine, greedy to have *this* inside her. If that meant coupling against a stone wall in the Marchioness of Sutton's garden, so be it. She would have him any way she could get him.

He groaned, and she smiled. Then he broke away, and she gasped in shock as they stood across from each other, cheeks flushed, panting, as if they'd raced all the way to Dover and back.

"We must stop," he said. "I'll ruin you, and I know that's not what you want."

Amelia blinked. "What?"

Ruin her? She was fairly certain she was already quite ruined.

"I won't risk the reputation you've worked so hard to reclaim."

She wasn't sure whether to laugh or cry. So, she did neither and simply stared at the dratted man.

"Here," he said, reaching out. "Your hair has gone quite askew."

She submitted while he attempted to fix her hair, her mind racing without a fixed destination, unable to form a tangible thought. Only seconds ago, he'd been about to make love to her against a wall, and it had felt so right. But this...

It felt wrong.

And she only had herself to blame.

He stepped back and assessed his work. "You might want to make straight for the ladies' retiring room. I'm afraid I've done more harm than good."

She nodded, silent, unable to trust herself to speak.

"We can't be seen returning together, so I'll take my leave now." He made a slight bow and continued around the side of the mansion.

It was only after he disappeared from view that a clear thought came to her.

She wanted to be ruined by Tristan.

The fact was she'd already ruined herself on him.

And she wanted to be ruined again.

What she no longer wanted was acceptance from the *haute ton*, but from one man.

Live in infamy with me.

He'd spoken those words to her, and she'd said no.

Tonight, a different answer came to her.
Tonight, she would plant her feet and fight for him.

Chapter Twelve

T RISTAN'S MANSION ON the opposite side of Grosvenor Square
came into view, and he wondered if he'd rambled about
London long enough to cool his blood.

He'd left the Marchioness of Sutton's ball without a fixed
destination and wandered about for nearly an hour before finding
himself back where he'd started the night, at Brooks's club. But
he'd lacked the appetite for booze, gambling, or company, so he'd
taken himself off on another ramble and now found himself
arriving home.

He'd nearly tupped Amelia against a wall.

That was the long and short of what would be haunting his
dreams—and his nightmares—on this and many more nights to
follow.

Certainly, he was known as the Dissolute Duke, but in truth,
there was nothing all that dissolute about him. Back in Italy, she'd
been correct on that score. He was no reprobate who gambled
away the family's fortune on a single toss of the dice. He was no
despoiler of virgins. Except...

He was.

And he wanted nothing more than to despoil her again.

Against a wall, if necessary.

Yet it wasn't only physical desire. In his experience, *that* typically cooled within days or weeks. Not so with Amelia. It was as if
the woman had entered his bloodstream, and the only cure for

her was more of her. Which only confirmed the obvious: she'd snuck past his defenses. She'd snuck past his fear of adoring another—of loving. He wasn't simply smitten like a green youth.

He was in love with that blasted, frustrating woman.

As he stepped onto the front landing of his house, the door swung wide. Thomas, his valet, had been waiting up for him. "Was it a good evening, sir?"

Tristan grunted and handed Thomas his hat and evening coat. Ready to be done with this night, he made straight for the staircase. Thomas cleared his throat, pointedly.

Tristan turned. "Is there something else?"

"Your," the valet began and appeared to have become stuck.

"Yes?" Tristan felt himself losing patience.

"Your, erm, *companion* awaits you in your studio."

Tristan's brow crinkled. "My companion?"

"She refused to give her name, but said you should be expecting her."

"You let an unknown woman inside my studio on the basis that she said I should be expecting her?" Had the world gone topsy-turvy?

Thomas splayed his hands wide in a gesture of helplessness. "The lady was quite determined."

And Tristan knew. This was no random woman, but...*Amelia*. Few could withstand her will. He shouldn't go too hard on Thomas. "In my studio?"

"Yes, sir."

Tristan's mind made up in a snap. "That will be all for the night, Thomas."

The valet gave a shallow bow and disappeared to his room.

Tristan only slowed his stride when he noticed the strip of orange light showing beneath the cracked door of his studio. Just beyond that door *she* waited for him. He tried to summon a healthy dose of pique to get him through whatever came next. She'd refused him, then kissed him blind in the Marchioness of Sutton's garden, giving him every indication she wanted more, tempting him to give her as much... And now she was here.

He wasn't sure how much more of Lady Amelia Windermere

he could take.

He pushed the door open on silent hinges and stepped inside the studio lit by a scattering of candles. Like a magnet, his gaze found her standing before a collection of statuettes he'd sculpted in his teen years. He observed her in profile, the straight nose, the stubborn chin. The way she took something in—fully, with the entirety of her attention. When one was the recipient of her gaze, one felt seen. It was a rare gift. Yes, one could be made uncomfortable when one didn't particularly want to be seen in a particular way, but on the other hand, it could make one feel special. He liked that about her.

He adored that about her.

He loved that about her.

He cleared his throat, and her head whipped around. She straightened and faced him, her gaze glinting with determination, but with something else, too, something he'd seen before...in Italy...in a fountain.

Recklessness.

He should brace himself.

"Have you been drinking prosecco?" He had to ask.

A smile curled about her mouth, and she shook her head. "No."

"Any other spirits?"

She laughed. "No."

He liked her laugh. He might adore it, too. Was there no end to his adoration for this woman? Now that he'd gotten the knack of it, he couldn't seem to stop.

He moved to his favorite armchair and sat down, his legs sprawled wide, indolent, as if her presence were an everyday occurrence. In truth, he'd done it to prevent himself from crossing the room and kissing her silly. Her lips were still lusciously kiss-crushed from earlier. "Would you like to tell me why you're here?" he asked, gruff.

She set down the small statuette she'd been inspecting and made her way to the charcoal-gray settee placed before the wide bow window dark with deep night. She perched on the plush velvet surface and flicked one, then the other, of her satin slippers off her feet before resting them to the side of her half-reclined body.

Anticipation quickened the beat of Tristan's heart. It couldn't help itself. She looked like a woman poised to be ravished.

"It occurred to me tonight," she said as if they were picking up in the middle of a conversation.

"What is that?"

"You and I never completed our bargain."

That blasted bargain. It should've never been agreed to in the first place. Yet he couldn't quite bring himself to regret it. In fact, he might make it again, given the chance. "You left Italy first, if you'll recall."

"Well, we're both in London now." Her mouth curved into the smile of a seductress. "We could finish what we started."

He crossed one ankle over a thigh. His half-staff cockstand was threatening to put on quite a show. "I should think you received all the material you need."

She lifted the hem of her dress, exposing the long, slender length of her legs up to her thighs. "Define *need*."

Twin shots of alarm and lust arrowed through him. "What are you—"

"I think it's only fair that I fulfill my side of the bargain." She slid one, then the other, stocking off her legs, allowing both to drift to the floor.

"Do not strip," he said with all the ducal authority he could muster, even as he understood this had nothing to do with anything as useless as a title. What lay between them had naught to do with their status as lord and lady, but as man and woman.

She swung her legs off the settee and came to her feet, now flicking open the mother-of-pearl buttons at the front of her dress, unhurried, one after the other, leaving him no choice but to watch, his mouth gone dry, a thin sheen of sweat pinpricking his skin.

"What will happen if I do?" she asked, disingenuous. One shoulder, then the other, shrugged and her dress fell to the floor, leaving her clad in naught but stays and chemise, its hem only just hiding her *mons pubis* from view.

Not so easily hidden? The cockstand demanding to be freed from his trousers.

He only just realized she'd asked a question, and he hadn't yet answered. Of course, there was but one answer. The truth. "I shall ravish you."

She took a few more steps as she reached behind her. The stays fell to the floor. "And what if I want to be ravished?"

He didn't have an answer. Not a proper one, anyway. Not one that held a shred of regard for the rules of society.

She lifted her chemise over her head and flung it away. She now stood naked—gloriously, unabashedly naked—before him, golden curls tumbling about her shoulders, hiding her sex from view, utterly tantalizing.

He dare not move.

All the moves were hers, anyway.

She closed the distance between them, shoving away the ankle that rested on his thigh, and stepped between his legs. His hands gripped the arms of the chair. They had no choice. They were either there or upon her.

She placed her hands upon his shoulders and leaned over him, her naked body only inches from his fully-clothed one. Yet he felt he was the exposed one. Her blonde curls tumbled about them. He breathed in her crisp lavender scent and another scent, too. *Woman.* He might burst from desire.

Soft lips feathered against the whorl of his ear. "What if I demand to be ravished?"

She brought her leg up so her shin stroked the length of his cock. As if to illustrate precisely with what she was demanding to be ravished.

How much more could a man take?

The answer was none.

On a low growl, he swept her into his arms and came to his feet. He caught her eye and held it. "Bloody hell, woman, if I'm to ravish you, then let's do it properly in a bed for once."

THE SENSE OF accomplishment she'd expected to feel at the Marchioness of Sutton's ball soared through Amelia now. Having convinced Tristan to ravish her felt more satisfying than a thousand invitations to a thousand balls.

As he carried her up a set of servant's stairs hidden behind the walls, she grabbed his face and kissed his mouth, breathing him in, reveling in the anticipation of what came next. She was exactly where she should be—wrapped in his arms, about to make love with him. She made quick work of his cravat and tossed it aside as they stepped inside a large room lit only by a low fire, sumptuously bedecked in dark, rich hues of saffron and mahogany. A massive four-poster bed stood in the middle.

His bedroom.

He deposited her on the plush, downy surface and stepped back, making short work of his clothing while she propped herself on her elbows and watched. With each article discarded her desire notched higher—waistcoat, boots, shirt, and trousers last, peeling them down those thick, rock-hard thighs of his.

Of course, his thighs weren't the only rock-hard part of his body.

A wave of raw lust channeled through her, and she was acting before she could think. She pushed forward, coming to her hands and knees, moving to the edge of the bed, reaching for his hips with one hand and for his manhood with the other, her fingers wrapping around his thick and, yes, *hard* length.

"Amelia, I…" he began and couldn't finish as she tugged him forward. Her gaze lifted and met his. His eyes had gone opaque, the pupils pushing his irises into silvery rings.

"'Tis *I* who shall be ravishing *you* tonight, Your Grace."

Her gaze holding his, her tongue stretched forward and stroked up the length of him. A long, animal groan poured from his parted mouth, and his head arced back. He tasted of salt and the musk specific to him. Again, she licked him. Again, he groaned.

Driven by instinct, she took him into her mouth, or as much as possible. There was just so much of him. His fingers wove through her hair, and his hips gave a shallow thrust. Gratification streaked through her at this giving of pleasure. How unexpected that it would make her body hum with wanting, too, but—*oh*—how her sex ached for *this* to be inside her as she stroked him with her mouth, his slick length sliding in and out. She'd never felt so empty in her life, so aching to be filled. She groaned from the denial, but it was the denial that stoked this desire into a lust like none she'd yet experienced.

She sucked him in deeper, and his hand began guiding her head. This give and take of control between them was unexpected, but not unwelcome. Only with him was she able to climb out of her mind and center her entire being in what was happening between her and another.

"Amelia," he muttered as if in pain, so great was his pleasure. "You must stop."

Her tongue swirled around the head of his manhood, and another groan poured from him. "Must I?"

He released her hair and reached beneath her chin. "*I* must stop," he said, and pulled away from her mouth, slowly, inch by inch. Oh, so many inches.

She rose to her knees, so they now faced each other. Dark intention in his eyes, he said, "Lie on your back."

Pure, animal lust shivered through her as she did as she was told. He grabbed her hips and pulled her to the edge of the bed, his hard manhood so slick against her quim she couldn't help squirming, leaving her legs no direction but up his body, a foot to either side of his head. He angled his face and kissed her instep as his hands tightened on her hips and he plunged inside her with a long, deep, possessive stroke. Oh, how he filled her. Desperate fingers clutched at the covers above her head, and she moaned. He stretched her to the point of pain, yet she angled her hips to receive more of him.

"You have the most perfect legs," he murmured against her ankle.

Nearly mindless, she squirmed against him, bringing him deeper, driven by a need that was now clawing at her. A need only he could satisfy. He met her gaze, and the playfulness fell away. He understood what her body craved as he began to drive into her with deliberation and intention, stoking this flame inside her higher and hotter.

"Oh, yes," she cried, the feeling catching her in its grip, winding her tighter, making her wild for him, her legs now wrapped around his waist, demanding more, demanding she give herself over to—to *him*. "Like *that*."

Of a sudden, all the world went dark and all its elements condensed where his sex met hers, provoking her to new heights of sensation. She met his gaze and, more profoundly, met connection there. All she felt, he felt, too. Not just the physical, but the spiritual, too. To the core of their souls.

One, then another stroke of his slick, long manhood, and she broke, all the light in the universe shot through her, sending stars through her veins, as her quim pulsed its climax around him.

"Amelia," he shouted, before pouring his release into her, his hands controlling the movement of her hips, the muscles of his chest and stomach contracting with the effort.

It was the most erotic view of Amelia's life.

Her view.

Hers.

That was who this man was.

Hers.

She wasn't sure who had claimed who, but the end result was the same: they belonged to each other.

He gathered her into his arms, remaining as one with her as they floated within the ether of satiety together. What they two shared...it was only for them. She never wanted to leave this place that only they knew. The rest of the world, with its demands and expectations, held no meaning in comparison.

And to think she'd convinced herself they did. To think she'd almost thrown all *this* away on a stubborn idea that held no true substance. The feel of this man in her arms... the weight of him pressed against her...the beat of their hearts one...

It was all that would ever matter.

He shifted his weight to the side, and they were no longer one. Her body already ached for him. He slid idle fingers through her curls, watching them slip through. She'd never felt more right. Her future was here, with this man. *Forever.*

She met his gray gaze, seeing the same satiety in there. "I never knew coupling could involve acrobatics," she said on a laugh. "My legs in the air like that."

A lazy half-smile tipped about his mouth. "Coupling can involve any number of acrobatics. We've only just started."

Twin frissons of desire and daring crept through her. She wouldn't mind adding to that number in a minute.

A seriousness entered his gaze, an inscrutability. It only made him more attractive. "I have a question for you."

Her breath caught in her chest. Here it was. The question she'd been waiting for him to ask—*again*—the answer—a different answer—poised on her lips. "Ask away," she said, breathless.

"Do you expect this to be a regular occurrence?"

A little laugh full of nerves escaped her. It wasn't quite the question she'd expected, but he would get there. "Oh, yes," she said.

Now if he would only ask that other question, for another *yes* was poised on her lips.

"How would you like to arrange it?" he asked.

Her brow crinkled. "Arrange it?"

What a strange way to ask her to marry him.

"That is generally how one manages a love affair," he said. "With an arrangement."

All the breath left her body. She wasn't sure she would ever be able to breathe again.

"Of course, there's another way to make it a regular occurrence."

"Which is?" she was somehow able to ask around the knot in her throat.

"Marriage." His gaze narrowed on her. "But I won't be asking you to marry me again."

"You won't?" Tears threatened. Oh, the shame.

He shook his head.

"Why not?" she asked. She might have demanded.

"It isn't what you want."

Knowledge landed on her with all the violence of a piano fallen from a great height.

He wouldn't be asking her to marry him.

Despair streaked through her. It was unreasonable, of course. She had refused him in Italy. But now they were in England. Now...

Oh, matters were different now.

She was different now.

"Unless..." he began, slowly, as if an idea was only now occurring to him.

"Yes?" she asked, impatient. The balance of her life felt in jeopardy.

His gaze bored into her, intense and questioning. "Unless you want me to ask you to marry me again."

Oh. She'd bungled everything. It wasn't Tristan who should be doing the asking.

It was she.

She gathered the coverlet still warm from their bodies and scrambled to her knees before sitting back onto her haunches. Tristan, on the other hand, gazed up at her from his prone position, unapologetically naked, slightly arrogant, and most definitely questioning. The urge to climb on top of him and make love to him again nearly overwhelmed her.

After.

She had to fix this—fix *them*—first.

"I have something to tell you," she said, "and I think it's best if we're both sitting for it." *So I don't ravish you again*, she didn't say.

He pushed to a seat and reclined against the headboard, pillows propped behind him. "Is this better?"

He reached for her, and she shook her head. "I can't be touching you and keep from ravishing you."

He chuckled. She didn't. It was only the truth.

She inhaled a deep, bracing breath. "I thought I wanted this one kind of life, and it was all I could imagine," she began. "I thought I wanted to be the *ton's* darling."

"I'm aware."

"I cared too much what others thought. That I only had value as long as I was valued by them."

"You hold so much more within you than that, Amelia."

The way he spoke those words—as statement of fact—burrowed deep inside her. She would never let them go as long as breath filled her lungs.

"It was you, Tristan, who showed me," she said. "You allowed me a glimpse of a different sort of life, one of possibility, and art, and desire, and acceptance, and... *love*." Tears sprang to her eyes. "I love you, Tristan. I only want to be your darling."

He took her hand and brushed the back of her fingers against his mouth. "You challenge me. You frustrate me. But never doubt this, Amelia. You are my love. You are my darling."

But she had more to say. "I only care what you think, and I love that you don't care what anyone in the world thinks."

He shook his head. "You are wrong there."

"I am?"

"You taught me to care what one other thinks. *You*." He sat forward and caressed her cheek. "Until you, I cared for nothing of value. Until you taught me the value of loving. I only want to adore you. I only want to love you. I only want *you*, the rest of the world be damned."

The freest laugh of her life sprang from Amelia. "The rest of the world be damned."

He pulled her close. But Amelia drew back from his kiss.

It was time.

"Tristan," she began.

"Yes?"

"I'll take you any way I can have you—as your mistress...as your slave."

His thumb brushed away the tear that broke free and rolled down her cheek. "As my wife will do."

She wasn't sure her heart could take much more. It was already so full. "Will you marry me, Tristan? Will you live in infamy with me for the rest of our days?"

Her heart in her throat, she waited for his answer.

"Being married will make us slightly less infamous," he said, conversationally, "but together we'll find a way." A laugh rumbled deep in his chest. "I think you'll take to infamy once you get the hang of it."

"You'll marry me?" He hadn't yet said yes.

"Yes, my love," he said. "You only had to ask."

And when he gathered her into his arms, and her lips met his, she knew that all they took on—life... love... making love— would be as art, because they made it so, together.

Epilogue

London
One year later

AMELIA STOOD IN her discreet corner and checked the gold pocket watch Tristan had given her as a wedding gift. Cheeky man.

Eight o'clock.

The doors to Sutton House would be opening any second. A frisson of anxiety flashed through her, and her palms slicked with sweat.

She'd insisted none of her family be here until the doors opened, like everyone else. *Everyone?* It might only be her family who showed up, and in truth, she might prefer it that way. Because what she was about to show the *ton*, well, they might not be prepared for it.

Oh, why had she agreed to a showing of her art?

Because Tristan had asked.

That was all.

And she could deny him nothing.

She took another sip of prosecco and smiled. Tristan had ordered it especially for the evening.

"What if I dance naked in a fountain?" she'd asked.

He'd given her the wicked smile that ever set her thighs ablaze. "This time I'll be able to enjoy it as your husband."

As attendees began to stream in, Amelia pasted the smile reserved for society onto her face and began extending greetings and thanks for their attendance at the Marchioness's little soirée in her honor. Naturally, her ears were attuned to any opinions of her work that might be floating on the air.

"There are certainly numerous studies of men's hands."

"Coarse hands," came another observation.

"The honest hands of a laborer," came yet another.

Amelia smiled a secret smile. Actually, she could inform them, if she were so inclined, they were the hands of a duke.

Her duke.

Further, she could tell them that she'd fallen in love with his hands first. Except that wasn't quite correct. She'd fallen in *lust* with his hands first, and the man himself not long after. *After* she'd experienced those hands on her body.

But it was a conversation starter that wasn't quite fit for polite company, and when she pulled back the curtains and revealed the triptych at the center of tonight's collection, she would be testing the limits of polite company quite far enough for one evening.

Through the set of open double doors leading from the next room strolled Archie, Delilah, and Juliet. Mama and Papa had returned from Samarkand early for her and Tristan's wedding, but then had immediately taken themselves off to Denmark.

Delilah took in the contents of the room with a sweeping glance. "There are certainly a lot of hands," she said. "I think it would be fair to say you have those down pat."

Amelia felt herself blushing at the gentle ribbing only her family could deliver.

"I take it those are the Duke's hands?" asked Juliet.

"They appear quite…" Archie began and stopped, as if only realizing his sister had painted those decidedly sensuous hands.

"*Capable*," finished Juliet, blushing.

It was true those hands could make a lady blush.

In fact, they did so on a regular basis.

As if the mention of him had conjured her muse into solid form, he strode into the room, catching no few pairs of eyes. Amelia had grown accustomed to the attention her husband's presence commanded. Not paying it one iota's worth of notice, he made straight for Amelia and wordlessly drew her in for a greeting kiss.

Her eyes opened when he pulled away, and she felt foolish. However fleeting, she ever gave herself over to her husband's kiss, reveling in the feeling of being deliciously claimed. A smile shone in his eyes. He knew. And his eyes promised more. *Later.*

Archie cleared his throat. "When's the big reveal, Amelia?" He checked his own pocket watch.

"Have somewhere to be, brother?" asked Delilah.

"It's Thursday, and Kilmuir is expecting me at the Five Graces."

Delilah snorted. "You and your low entertainments."

"Ah, they're good fun, Lilah. You should join us one night."

Delilah's eyes went wide in a perfect affectation of shock. "What? And destroy my speckless reputation?"

Again, Amelia accepted her family's ribbing. They understood where she now stood on the matter of reputation and its importance.

With them.

On the side of infamy.

Speaking of which, the time had nearly arrived to cast that reputation firmly in stone.

"Duchess," came the Marchioness of Sutton's cultured voice, "are you ready for the unveiling of your *pièce de resistance?*" Her gaze flicked toward Tristan. "Ripon, I never knew your hands were quite so...commanding." The marchioness blushed like a girl several decades her junior.

"I'm ready," said Amelia with a show of bravado, though she quaked on the inside.

The marchioness nodded and mingled into the considerable crowd that had gathered, leaving Tristan and Amelia a moment to themselves.

She caught his gaze. "Are you ready?"

His eyes glinted with mischief. "Are you?"

"As I'll ever be."

The crowd followed the marchioness's progress toward the curtained centerpiece of the showing. "I must thank everyone for coming out tonight in support of a most promising new artist, the Duchess of Ripon. Without further ado, I present *Man in Three*

Moods: A Study." She signaled a servant, who drew the curtain back.

A few seconds of studied silence...

A collective gasp...

Several more seconds of stunned, scandalized silence.

Before the collective hung three paintings of the Duke of Ripon in various poses...all while starkly, unrepentantly nude. From left to right: the first in the style of a traditional portrait with him facing the viewer squarely with his typical expression of dukely arrogance; the second a silhouette of his body, his head angled just enough to reveal a wicked smile on his mouth and in his eyes; and the third...that was the one which likely had the room growing hotter in their clothes. He lay on his back, an arm draped above his head, utterly and completely spent, his direct gaze replete with satiety.

Amelia remembered that session well.

Now, Tristan reached for her hand and squeezed. "Steady on," he murmured. "Everyone came here to be treated to your art."

"But I have a feeling they'll be staying to ogle your naked form," she said, dry.

The twinkle in his eyes invited her into a conspiracy with him. "Artistically rendered, of course."

It was true, for his, ahem, manhood was tastefully angled out of view. To show it, would've been one step too far into infamy for Amelia.

She snorted. Her husband had taught her well. She might be a novelty of an artist—*a duchess!*—but he might rival her as a nude model—*a duke!*

A few attendees stalked out of the room, thunderstorms on their faces, the word dissolute trailing in their wake; others planted their feet and canted their heads in study. Whether it was down to Tristan's rather impressive nude form or her ability as a watercolorist, she didn't know or care.

"Sister," said Delilah, leaning in to murmur into Amelia's ear, "who knew that *you* would become the most scandalous Windermere of us all?"

An easy laugh escaped Amelia, the sort of laugh she'd never been capable of before meeting Tristan. "I'm quite certain that if you put your mind to it, you could top me, Lilah."

A pensive expression on her face, Delilah returned her attention to the triptych.

"And you, dear husband," Amelia began, sliding her arm through Tristan's, snugging close.

"Yes?"

"When shall you exhibit your latest works?"

His gaze turned serious. "Those are not, nor ever will be, for the public's consumption, my sweet."

They were speaking, of course, of the set of nude sculptures Tristan had done of her this spring. Now that she thought about it, she really would prefer all and sundry didn't know the particular shape of her breasts or the indent of her navel.

The simple fact was they couldn't get enough of each other.

They were each other's muses.

They were each other's obsession.

No shortage of shocked glances continued to be thrown their way. If this was what it felt like to be infamous—wildly and completely alive—then she looked forward to a lifetime of infamy with this man.

"You are my forever love, Tristan."

Oh, the words she found herself saying to this man on a daily basis.

"I'll hold you to it."

And he took her in his arms before all gathered and kissed her until her head went giddy and her knees weak, thereby sealing their reputation as the most dissolute, indiscreet couple of the *ton*.

The End

About the Author

Sofie Darling is an award-winning author of historical romance. The third book in her Shadows and Silk series, Her Midnight Sin, won the 2020 RONE award for Best Historical Regency.

She spent much of her twenties raising two boys and reading every romance she could get her hands on. Once she realized she simply had to write the books she loved, she finished her English degree and embarked on her writing career. Mr. Darling and the boys gave her their wholehearted blessing.

When she's not writing heroes who make her swoon, she runs a marathon in a different state every year, visits crumbling medieval castles whenever she gets a chance, and enjoys a slightly codependent relationship with her beagle, Bosco.

CPSIA information can be obtained
at www.ICGtesting.com
Printed in the USA
BVHW031232260722
643033BV00014B/846